SO-BJK-986

NO GOD IN SAGUARO

Other books by Lewis B. Patten

GUNS AT GRAY BUTTE

PROUDLY THEY DIE

GIANT ON HORSEBACK

THE ARROGANT GUNS

"Are you leaving on the stage?" the sheriff asked.

"No. I know what happened to my brother Jess. But I still don't know why. I think that before I leave I want to know the whole dirty story. I owe him that much."

The sheriff opened his mouth to speak, then scowled and shut it again. Any explanation would sound weak. He said, "Suppose I told you the whole story? Would you leave?"

Lane Sauer shook his head. There was both anger and contempt in his eyes, but he did not speak.

"Why? Is it revenge you want?"

"Maybe. I don't know. All I can think about is Jess, choking, his face turning red, then blue. All I can think about is the people of this town, doing that to him for something he hadn't even done."

"They'll kill you, Sauer. They'll kill you the way they killed him."

 LOOK FOR THE DOUBLE D BRAND

NO GOD
IN SAGUARO

LEWIS B. PATTEN

1966
DOUBLEDAY & COMPANY, INC., GARDEN CITY, NEW YORK

All of the characters in this book are fictitious,
and any resemblance
to actual persons, living or dead,
is purely coincidental.

Library of Congress Catalog Card Number 66–12226
Copyright © 1966 by Lewis B. Patten
All Rights Reserved
Printed in the United States of America
First Edition

NO GOD IN SAGUARO

WITHDRAWN

WITHDRAWN

CHAPTER 1

At high noon the stage wheeled precariously around a sharp turn at the top of a barren ridge and began its descent to the desert floor over a series of switchbacks that the driver negotiated with practiced but hair-raising ease. Inside, Lane Sauer, his face shining with sweat and grimed with dust, looked out at the muddy surface of the sluggish river and at the town of Saguaro, scattered untidily along its bank.

The fat little whisky drummer across from him did not bother to raise his head. The tall, rawboned man on his left stared unseeingly, almost gloomily at the floor between his knees.

Frowning lightly, Lane glanced across the rock-strewn slope, upon which nothing grew but a few browning, giant saguaros and fewer, equally dry barrel cactuses. At the foot of the slope the town seemed deserted in the noonday heat. Here was where his brother had disappeared, he thought, the place from which his last letter had come more than six months before. Here was the place from which he must start his search. He raised his glance, looking beyond both town and river at the desert, disappearing in shimmering horizon and brassy sky. Was Jess out there, picked clean by buzzards, his bones bleaching in the

1

sun? He shook his head almost imperceptibly as though to clear it of that unwelcome thought.

The coach entered town without slackening its speed. It raised a giant cloud as it rattled along the broad, dusty street; and when it stopped with a great clatter of plunging hoofs and squeaking thorough braces, the dust cloud rolled forward and enveloped it.

Lane opened the door and climbed stiffly out. His rump was sore from the endless miles of pounding the coach had given it and his muscles ached. Blinking in the dazzling sunlight, he stepped to the weathered boardwalk and waited for his carpetbag to be unloaded from the boot.

The whisky drummer climbed out wearily and mopped at his streaming face with a soiled handkerchief. His suit was rumpled and there was a red line around his fat neck where his celluloid collar had rubbed.

The other man followed. He was dressed in range clothes and scuffed boots. His shirt, Union Army issue, was faded on the shoulders and back to a dingy gray. Sweat had left a white stain of salt at his armpits and down both sides of his back. He glanced at Lane without fully meeting his eyes, then stepped to the rear of the coach to wait for his bag to be handed down.

Lane studied him carefully now, and the man, aware of his scrutiny, frowned. But he did not raise his glance. The driver handed him his bag and the man tramped away down the street, clutching it. He had introduced himself to Lane as Nicolo Finch fifty miles or so back where he had boarded the coach. But as soon as Lane shook his hand his friendliness disappeared and he lapsed into silence, afterward staring steadily at the floor between his feet.

The driver tossed Lane's bag to the boardwalk and he picked it up. He followed the whisky drummer into the

2

hotel. Over his shoulder the man grumbled, ". . . don't know why I had to draw this lousy, God-forsaken territory."

The lobby was relatively cool. A faint odor of cooking cabbage hung in the air, mingling with the smell of stale cigar smoke. There were a couple of leather-covered sofas and several chairs. Beyond was a desk with the inevitable rack of pigeonholes behind it and a brass spittoon in front.

The clerk glanced at Lane, his eyes briefly startled, as though he had unexpectedly glimpsed someone he knew. He looked quickly away and gave his attention to the whisky drummer, who signed the dog-eared register and accepted his key sullenly as though the heat and the coach ride were the clerk's personal responsibility.

Lane stepped up behind him, reached for the register and stub of pencil and signed his name. The clerk looked down at it. The signature held his gaze longer than seemed necessary so Lane asked, "Something the matter?"

The man, middle-aged and bald, glanced up. He seemed to be sweating more than he had been before. "No. Of course not. I'll give you number five. Head of the stairs on your left."

Lane took the key, picked up his dusty carpetbag and tramped toward the stairs. They creaked as he climbed them.

His room was the first one beyond the head of the stairs. He unlocked the door, went in, removed the key and closed the door. He took off his hat and sailed it at the bed.

The best place to begin, he thought, would be the post office, for that was where Jess's last letter had been mailed. Maybe the postmaster would remember him. But it could wait until evening, when the street would be

3

cooler than it was right now. A long stage ride in this awful, searing heat took the starch right out of a man.

There was a pitcher of tepid water on the bureau. He poured the wash pan half full and washed his face. He got a comb from the bag and ran it through his short, coarse black hair. His face was red from the heat and there was a two-day stubble of black whiskers on his lean, sunburned jaws.

His gray eyes looked calmly around the room, at the chipped paint on the furniture, at the sagging, lumpy mattress on the bed. He crossed to the window and, eyes narrowed slightly against the glare, stared down into the street. He saw the hotel clerk, in shirt sleeves, black sleeve-protectors and green eyeshade, hurrying along the walk. The man went into a square stone building across the street. The windows of the building had bars on them.

Lane's eyes changed almost imperceptibly and he felt a quickening of his pulse. It might be coincidence that the clerk was running to the local law so soon after his arrival here. It also might not.

He waited at the window until the hotel clerk reappeared, not hurrying as much as he had before. Approaching the hotel, the man glanced up, saw Lane and quickly glanced down again.

Lane left the window, crossed the room and lay down on the bed. He stared at the ceiling unblinkingly, at a spot where something, a bullet perhaps, had knocked a chunk of plaster out.

Already he knew one thing. The name Sauer was not unknown in Saguaro. Nicolo Finch had recognized it. So had the hotel clerk. He began to wonder if Jess had gotten into trouble here. He also wondered why he had not questioned Finch in the coach during the long ride, why he had not asked the clerk if he knew Jess when

4

the man had so obviously seen the family resemblance as he glanced at him.

He frowned faintly. He didn't know what had kept him silent, but something had. He guessed it didn't really matter. There was plenty of time for questions when the air grew cool with coming night.

He closed his eyes, remembering his brother Jess, remembering the reckless, laughing glint that had sometimes been in his brother's eyes, the rebellion that had been in him too, wanting to do something on his own without the weight and power of the Sauer clan to back him up.

Clan was the proper word for the Sauers, thought Lane. Over in the Texas Panhandle everybody knew the name. They knew the crusty old man, who had settled the place in spite of Comanche and Kiowa and had held it against all comers while his sons were being born and growing up. They also knew that when you tackled one of the Sauers, you tackled all of them because that was the way they were.

The family had a single bank account, against which any member could draw without restraint, without question or censure, no matter what the amount he drew. Into the bank account went the earnings of the ranch and the earnings of the individual family members if they worked or engaged in business ventures outside the confines of the ranch. This, Lane realized, helped give the family its extraordinary unity. They were truly all for one and one for all.

They had understood Jess's reasoning when he went away. But he had been missed and whenever one of his letters arrived the whole clan had gathered, grouped around the old man to listen as he read it in his impatiently halting way.

Lane got up nervously, the bed creaking thunderously

as he did. He began to pace back and forth, unmindful now of the ever-present heat. He was sweating and he crossed to the window to open it.

There seemed to be more activity in the street, and one thing was strange. All those in the street were men. Lane saw neither women nor children there.

The mercantile store, over which hung a sign reading, "Holt Childers—General Merchandise," seemed to be enjoying all the business. It was into this store that all the men in the street eventually disappeared.

Lane frowned puzzledly. A faint, hot breeze now blew in the open window, stirring the dusty curtains as it did. He left the window and crossed to his bag, which was resting on the floor. He knelt, reached in and withdrew his holstered revolver and cartridge belt. For a moment he hesitated, then returned gun and belt to the bag and snapped it shut.

Impatience was pushing him and a new, unaccustomed uneasiness. It was as though this town, even the inanimate part of it, was hostile to him the way the desert is hostile to certain kinds of life. He could feel it in the room, in the walls, in the air that drifted through the open window. He could feel it when he looked down into the street.

He began to pace again, thinking unaccountably of a time when he was a boy, of an evening he had felt this same hostility in the air, in the very land around the ranch house. He remembered, too, the screaming Comanche attack that had come with the dawn.

He knew now that there had been actual human hostility then, even though there had been no evidence of it. And there was actual human hostility here, a thing he felt but could not see.

Abruptly, he picked up his hat off the bed and put it

on. He left the room, locking the door and pocketing the key.

He went briskly down the stairs. He glanced at the hotel desk as he went through the lobby, but no one was there. The lobby itself was deserted.

He stepped out into the street. The coach was gone but there were two fresh piles of droppings to show where it had stood. Lane glanced up and down the street. Nothing moved. It was as though the town suddenly was dead, its people gone, its breathing stilled. In spite of the heat, Lane suddenly felt a chill, a stirring of goose flesh along his arms and on the back of his neck.

Impatiently he shook his head and strode off down the street. He had no idea where the post office was but he knew he could find it if he looked.

He walked all the way to the end of the street, to the riverbank, noticing as he did that the town seemed to be sharply divided into two segments by a cross street just below the hotel. The upper half, no doubt built later than the lower half, was as well kept as the rest was run down. The hotel in which he was staying was on the corner, across from a large store that combined furniture, hardware and undertaking on the ground floor, that apparently provided office space on the second floor.

Between this hotel and another one, closer to the river, there were only weed-grown vacant lots, littered with trash and rusting tin cans. Between the river and the second hotel, on the same side of the street, there was a feed and seed store. Lane wondered wryly what the hell they could get to grow in this desert heat.

Diagonally across from his own hotel was a gunsmith shop. Nearer the river there were two saloons, the jail and three run-down houses with sagging fences that looked like cribs. Next to them was a towering yellow livery barn with corrals out back and thirty or forty wheeled vehicles of various kinds parked alongside of it.

Lane stood on the riverbank, looking out, thinking that it was a wonder the water didn't just turn to steam. There was no bridge but apparently there was a shallow ford because wheel tracks disappeared into the water and emerged again on the other side.

He packed and lighted his pipe and stood there staring uptown at the empty street for a long, long time. His face was sharp-lined and roughhewn in spite of the softening effect of the two-day growth of beard. His brows, as black as his beard, were heavy above deep-sunken eyes that could be as hard as granite chips. But there was a quality about his mouth—a tipping of the corners with the hint of ever-present humor and a fullness out of keeping with the rest of his face that made those who saw him wonder involuntarily what he would be like when he smiled.

He slowly retraced his steps and now he saw the townsmen pouring out of Holt Childers' mercantile store uptown and diagonally across the street from the hotel. They dispersed quickly and the street was virtually empty again by the time he had reached the hotel. Obviously there had been some kind of town meeting, attended only by the men.

Still looking for the post office, he went on. He found it next to the hotel, set back from from the walk by a dozen feet and combined with the office of the stage line. Beyond it there was a grocery store and a hardware store. Across the street there was another saloon, called the Uptown, a dry-goods store and, between that and Holt Childers' mercantile, a small dressmaker's shop.

Lane went to the post office and opened the door. The man behind the barred grille jerked his head around to look at him almost guiltily. Lane said with a touch of irritation in his voice, "I'm Lane Sauer. We got a letter from my brother with this postmark six months ago. We haven't heard from him since and I'm looking for him. Can you tell me anything?"

The man's hands lay on the counter, brown as old parchment, blue-veined and trembling. He stared down at them as he said defensively, "Sauer? Sauer? I don't seem to remember anyone by that name. A lot of letters get mailed here—by saddletramps driftin' through. Man can't keep track of all of 'em."

Lane stared at the man's face. It was old and gaunt. His head was thatched with thin white hair. He said shortly, "Thanks," and wheeled away. He went out the door without looking back, turned at the walk and entered the hotel. The clerk was behind the desk again and two men were standing there talking to him.

Puzzled and for the moment balked, Lane climbed the stairs to his room. Something was wrong here in this town. Something was wrong and it had to do with Jess. He knew that as well as he'd ever known anything.

He crossed the room and picked up his bag. He opened it and reached inside for his gun and cartridge belt, troubled by some elusive change in the bag itself.

His hand encountered only his clothes, his razor and shaving soap. And he knew what elusive thing had puzzled him. The bag had been too light. His gun and cartridge belt were gone.

CHAPTER 2

For several moments Lane stood there, utterly still, his eyes turned hard as bits of stone. He had locked the room. The door had not been forced. Whoever had taken his gun had entered with a key.

His first inclination was to storm downstairs and confront the clerk, but he did not yield to it. Instead he crossed the room and stared thoughtfully down into the street.

Again the menace of this town seemed tangible, a solid thing he could feel, could almost touch, but could not see. And now he was unarmed, without the means to defend himself against whatever unknown thing was hostile toward him.

He began to pace back and forth, a light frown on his face. What would they expect of him now? The frown faded slowly. They'd expect him to come stamping downstairs demanding to know why his room had been entered and his personal belongings tampered with. He'd do the opposite. He'd pretend he didn't know anything about the theft.

Furthermore, he would wait a while before he showed himself. Let them worry when he did not appear. Let them wonder what was keeping him.

He fumbled in his bag until he had located his shaving things. He crossed to the bureau again.

He dumped the basin into the slop jar on the floor, then refilled it and began lathering his face. He hung the razorstrop on the hook screwed into the wall for that purpose and began to strop his razor. He lathered again and began to shave.

Finished, he wiped his face, cleaned the razor and dried it, then dumped the water and crossed to his carpetbag. He took out a clean shirt and put it on. He went to the window again.

The street looked more normal now. A dog sidled along in the thin strip of shade cast on the walk by the buildings across the street. Two barefoot boys came shuffling along in the dry dust of the street behind the dog. A woman went into Holt Childers' mercantile. A man came out of the Uptown Saloon, felt the blast of heat in the street and retreated into the saloon again.

Lane turned, crossed the room and locked the door. He left the key in the lock. He stretched out on the bed and closed his eyes. His body was tense, his muscles tight. He began to review all that had happened so far.

Doing so, he realized that few of the things he had felt were definite. Finch's attitude had seemed strange but, viewed by itself and objectively, could have been nothing more than irritation caused by the heat and the jolting motion of the coach. The clerk and the postmaster had also seemed to act strangely but again he admitted it might have been his imagination working overtime. As for the feeling of menace emanating from tangible things in the town . . . He smiled ruefully to himself. That could be purely imagination. Only the theft of the gun was real and even that might mean nothing more than that the hotel maid was a thief.

He could buy another gun easily enough so the loss wasn't serious. And he would probably discover that he'd been imagining things, about the town, about the people he'd encountered so far. He'd try and sleep through the worst heat of the afternoon. Later, when it was cooler, he'd go down to the jail and see if the sheriff knew anything about Jess.

The heat seemed even more oppressive than it had before. He found himself remembering home, five hundred miles away.

The house back home was built like a fort, backed up against a low hill, dug into it and therefore cool even on the hottest days. Its walls were of adobe and were more than two feet thick. The windows were barred and so narrow that an arrow or bullet would have to be fired from directly in front of the house to come on through. A well, dug before the house was built, was beneath the floor of the huge living room so that water would be available to the defenders no matter how long the house was under siege. And, dug back into the hill itself, there was a root cellar filled with enough provisions to last for several months.

The roof was of sod, nearly two feet thick, supported by great, thick spruce poles and brush.

And the land . . . It was not like this. It was not desert and baking, barren rock but grass that in spring and summer rippled in the wind like the waves of some limitless inland sea. Out on the grass were cattle, long-horned Texas cattle that could stand the summer's heat, that grew long, shaggy coats in winter to protect them from the northers and ice storms that occasionally howled down out of the high country to the north and west.

A noisy place, the Sauer ranch, a place that rang with

men's shouts, where horseplay and rough humor enlivened the loneliness . . .

Lane dropped off to sleep, to dream that he was still riding in the coach. The feeling of movement, of motion, was very real. He awoke, and slept again, and when he awakened the second time the sun was low in the western sky.

He got up, washed his sweaty face and combed his hair. His clothes were soaked with sweat.

He remembered the gun and a feeling of unwelcome uneasiness touched his mind. He put on his hat, crossed to the door, unlocked it and went out. He locked it behind him and pocketed the key.

He went slowly down the stairs and, though he felt the eyes of the desk clerk watching him, did not turn his head. He crossed the lobby and went out into the street.

He paused there for a moment, squinting against the glare of the sinking sun. Then he headed toward the jail.

A breeze stirred, blowing out of the hilly country east of town. Evaporation of the sweat on his shirt cooled Lane for the first time today. Perhaps it was this that caused the faint chill he felt. He dragged his huge silver watch from his pocket and opened the case. It was a little before seven o'clock.

He angled across the street toward the jail. It was a dismal-looking building even in the light of day. Built of native stone, it was dun-colored like the dust in the street. There were two large, dirty windows in front and a heavy plank door, strapped with iron. A sign, nailed to the door, said: SHERIFF. SAGUARO COUNTY.

Lane opened the door. It was cooler inside but the air was musty and smelled of stale cigar smoke. There was a barred door on the far side of the room which led to the cells at the rear. There was a cot and a roll-top desk, untidily littered with papers.

Lane called, "Anybody here?" and got no reply. He turned back to the door and went through it into the street. There was a bench beside the door and he sat down on it.

Up at the corner he saw a man come into view and head toward the jail. He knew instantly that this was the sheriff, for the badge was visible on his shirt.

He was a heavy-set man dressed in boots and tight cavalry pants from which the yellow stripes had been removed, leaving a darker strip of unfaded material visible beneath. His shirt was butternut color and looked like homespun material to Lane. Reaching Lane, he stopped and said, "You want to see me?"

Lane got up and stuck out his hand. He had always thought of his hand as being large, but the sheriff's almost enveloped it. Lane said, "I'm Lane Sauer."

"Burt Manus. I'm the sheriff. You must be the stranger that came in on the stage."

Lane thought, "You know damned well who I am," but he only nodded his head. He studied the sheriff, who had shoved his hat back away from his gleaming forehead.

As far as Lane could see, he was completely bald except for a fringe of coarse gray hair at his temples and on the back of his neck. Above the tanned line where his hat had been, his skin was white. His mouth was heavy, wide, but strong and humorless. His chin jutted out below it like a rock. His eyes, wide-set beneath a pair of the heaviest, thickest brows Lane had ever seen, were pale blue, and hard, and, Lane thought, a little bit wary too. Lane said, "It's about my brother Jess. We got a letter from him sent from here more'n six months ago. We haven't heard from him since. I wondered if you knew anything . . . if you remembered him."

The sheriff frowned but he did not immediately reply. Lane said, "And I want to report a theft. My gun was stolen from my room in the hotel. The lock wasn't broken. Whoever stole it used a key."

Manus' pale eyes stared unblinkingly at him, as though trying to probe his thoughts. He said, "I'll see what I can find out about the gun, but I don't know anything about your brother. A lot of drifters go through here. Chances are he headed out across the desert and got lost. There are a lot of bones out there."

Lane didn't know how he knew, but he did. The sheriff had lied to him. Burt Manus, like the postmaster, remembered Jess. Lane said, "Funny."

"What's funny?"

"That a man can come into a town, write a letter and mail it, maybe buy supplies for the trip across the desert, and still nobody remembers him. Do you get that many strangers here?"

The sheriff's eyes turned cold as ice. He stared steadily at Lane for several moments. When he spoke, his voice was clipped and harsh. "I'll overlook that, mister, but just this once. Don't call me a liar again."

Lane shrugged. "I'll be at the hotel when you find my gun."

"Don't figure on staying too long."

Lane turned and walked away, frowning to himself. The sun was now down below the horizon. A feeling of helplessness and frustration washed through him. He felt as he once had as a small boy when his brothers took his new hat and made a game of keeping it away from him. Wherever he turned, he met with failure, for the hat sailed over his head into the waiting hands of another of his brothers, who in turn sailed it to another when he turned that way. The game had gone on interminably while rage and frustration grew in Lane. The angrier he got the more they laughed.

Perhaps, he thought, he should terminate this the way he'd ended that game so long ago. He'd tackled Luke, his oldest brother, like a small wildcat, fighting fiercely until Luke retreated. Then he had attacked Matt, who was holding the hat at the time. In the end they'd shame-facedly given him his hat and they'd never tormented him that way again.

At the corner he saw a man come out of the furniture, hardware and undertaking establishment across the street and on impulse stopped and spoke to him. "Can you tell me where the cemetery is?"

The man was tall and, Lane judged, in his thirties. He was dressed in black and had a thin, solemn face. He jerked his head around and stared briefly at Lane. He cleared his throat and swallowed. He gestured vaguely toward the south. "Edge of town, that way." He turned away hurriedly and crossed the street, almost running, looking neither to right nor left.

Lane watched him go. Something was very wrong in this town. Everyone he met, everyone he spoke to acted strangely toward him. He turned abruptly and headed south.

This, he judged, was the Mexican section of town. Frame construction gave way to adobe. A couple of dogs came out from beside one of the shacks and barked at his heels. A dark-faced woman turned her head and stared at him impassively.

He saw children, but no other adults. Yet he felt as though he was being watched.

He followed the street he was on and, after traveling a couple of blocks, reached the edge of the town. The cemetery was only a cleared patch of desert in which a few headstones were visible. There were also a number of wooden crosses, some of them painted white. He guessed there were thirty or forty graves in all.

The afterglow of the setting sun put an orange light on the land. He walked among the crosses, reading names. He did not expect to find his brother's name.

At the far side of the cemetery were the newer graves. Here, the earth was lightly mounded over each one. And here, all the graves but two had markers on them. He stopped before these unmarked ones, staring down at them.

He found himself remembering Jess, remembering his brother's face so clearly Jess might have been standing here looking at him. And he wondered if Jess was one of the nameless ones lying here.

Abruptly he wheeled and strode back toward the town, now lying gray and still in the gathering dusk. The dogs came out and barked at his heels and a soft voice called them away in Spanish. Lane whirled and approached the house from which the voice had come. He said, "*Buenas noches, señor.*"

The voice acknowledged the greeting. Lane could see the man now, squatting against the adobe wall. Lane knew Spanish almost as well as he knew English. Swiftly, in Spanish, he queried the man about his brother.

The silence afterward was complete. The dogs had stopped barking. The sounds coming from the houses had also stopped. Even the children seemed to have stopped their play.

The man's voice was scarcely more than a whisper when it came. "I know nothing of your brother, *señor*. No doubt he left Saguaro after posting his letter to you. Look beyond this town for him, *señor*, for you will not find him here."

"*Muchas gracias*," Lane murmured, and turned toward the center of the town. Behind him the silence was unbroken.

CHAPTER 3

There was a light in the gunsmith's shop when he passed
it on the way to the hotel. He tried the door and found
that it was unlocked.

He went in and closed the door behind him. The place
was divided by a partition running the width of the shop.
A door in the partition opened into the rear half of the
building and there was a counter in front of it. Behind
the counter the wall was covered with gunracks in which
rifles and shotguns stood, and with nails upon which
tagged revolvers hung.

A man came through the door, looked expectantly at
Lane, then looked away with a completely altered expression when he saw who it was. Lane said drily, "Yeah. It's
me. I'd like to buy a gun."

The man glanced at him, frowning suddenly. He was
short, squat and powerful, with a head that seemed too
large for the rest of him. He wore overalls and a leather
apron like those Lane had seen blacksmiths wear. He had
a brown, clipped mustache and beard, and seemed preoc-
cupied.

Lane repeated, "I want to buy a gun."

"A new gun? I'm afraid I don't have any I can sell to

you. Most of my work is repair work." He gestured toward the wall at his back.

Lane said, "Or you don't want to sell me one. Could that be it?"

"I don't know what you're talking about. Just a minute. I'll see what I've got out back."

He went through the door leading to the rear of the shop. A moment later, Lane heard the alley door softly close.

Irritation was stirring in him, coupled with a strengthened belief that everyone in Saguaro knew more about Jess than they wanted to admit. And for the first time, he felt a threat here in this town, a threat against his own safety, perhaps even against his life.

He supposed he could simply take a gun and leave enough money for it on the counter. He moved to go around the counter, then stopped himself. Taking a gun would be playing deliberately into their hands. The money he had left for it would probably disappear and the sheriff would arrest him for theft. Perhaps the same thing that had happened to Jess would happen to him.

He turned back to the window, scowling angrily, surprised at his own thoughts. Why was he so sure something had happened to Jess? Why this sudden, dismal certainty?

Faintly he could hear the noise from the saloon next door. He wondered where the gunsmith had gone and how soon he would be back.

He did not have to wonder long. The sheriff opened the street door and stepped inside, followed by the gunsmith, who left the door standing wide. The sheriff said in his deep, harsh voice, "Murphy here tells me you're trying to buy a gun. You figuring on shooting somebody?"

"Carrying a gun isn't against the law."

"No. It ain't against the law. Startin' trouble is, and I figure you're tryin' to start trouble here. I told Frank not to sell you one."

"And I suppose you won't try very hard to recover mine."

The sheriff's eyes narrowed. He started to speak, then clamped his mouth tightly shut.

Lane thought that, under different circumstances, he would have liked this man. Now he could feel his anger grow, fed by a frustration he seemed unable to overcome. He said, "It won't work, Sheriff. You can't get rid of me. I'll stay here until I find out what I want to know."

"Don't push it, son. I can get rid of you any time I want. And I think maybe that'll be on tomorrow's stage."

Lane stared coldly at him. "That's where we disagree. I'm not leaving until I find out what happened here."

He could see that what he'd said had struck a nerve. Burt Manus turned heavily and went out the door. He spoke over his shoulder in a flat, implacable voice. "The stage tomorrow. You be on it, son."

Lane glanced at the gunsmith, Frank. The man looked acutely uncomfortable. Lane said, "There's a new grave over at the cemetery but there's no marker on it. Who's buried there?"

The man swallowed, then glared angrily at Lane. "How the hell should I know? Now get out of here and leave me be. I got work to do." He went behind the counter and put a hand under it.

Lane went out the door. After a moment he heard it slammed behind him, heard the key turn in the lock. He was hungry now and realized he'd had nothing to eat since morning. He crossed the street to the hotel and went into the dining room. Several people were eating, but none of them looked at him, a fact that struck him as peculiar since he was a stranger and since everyone else seemed to know who he was. He sat down at a table near the door.

A pretty Mexican girl was waiting on tables. She ignored him. Half an hour passed. At last he got up and crossed the dining room to her. "Guess you didn't see me, ma'am. I'd like something to eat."

Fright was in her eyes as she looked at him. Her voice was thin with it. "I'm sorry. We're closed."

"What about them?" He gestured toward the others.

"They . . . they were here before we closed."

Lane nodded. He went back through the lobby and out into the street. His anger was growing steadily and he didn't even try to keep it in check. Maybe one of the saloons, he thought. Maybe a free lunch counter in one of the saloons . . .

Across the street, the gunsmith's shop was dark. The saloon next to it seemed to be the busiest of the three in town. He could see the bartender of the third saloon, down next to the jail, sitting in a tilted chair on the walk outside.

Funny, he thought, that one saloon would be so busy, the one next to it deserted and without a customer. He crossed the street and entered the busy one, which, according to its sign, was called Dutch's.

Silence spread away from him like waves spreading from a pebble tossed into a lake. It lasted for perhaps ten seconds. Then the noise resumed again. Lane crossed to the bar. There was a free lunch counter at its end. He ordered a beer, and while the bartender drew it, walked down to the lunch counter and filled a plate. He returned, paid for the beer, picked it up and carried it to a vacant table at the rear of the room.

Everything but that sudden silence had been normal

22

enough, he thought. And yet, he knew every man in the saloon was watching him.

He ate hungrily, washing the food down with beer. He stared around the room, not missing the way eyes shifted from watching him, the way stilled conversations resumed. This was incredible, he thought. Or else it was pure imagination on his part.

He finished his beer and took the glass to the bar for another one. Men began to leave, singly and in twos and threes. By the time he had reached his table again, the saloon was half empty. The bartender was scowling at him as though he'd like to slit his throat.

He drank the beer slowly and finished his free lunch. More men left until at last only three remained. One of these was the postmaster. Another was the gunsmith. The third he didn't know.

He got up and slowly crossed to where they sat. He said without smiling, "You'd think I had leprosy or something, wouldn't you?"

Something was different in the way they looked at him. Both the postmaster and the gunsmith, Frank Murphy, had seemed afraid of him before. Now their eyes mirrored something else, something close to hate.

The third man, dark, glowering and powerful, said, "Mister, you've got something worse than leprosy. You could even die from it."

Lane looked at Murphy. "Who's he?"

"Otto Riker." The man spoke for himself, his voice deep and hoarse. "I'm the blacksmith."

Lane said, "Everybody's sure scared. They jump every time I say my brother's name. Why do you suppose that is?" Every nerve in his body was tense, every muscle taut.

23

Riker said, "Get out of town, mister. Do what Burt Manus told you to. Be on the stage tomorrow."

Lane shook his head. "Huh-uh. Not for a while. There's a bad smell in this town and I think I'll find out what's making it."

Riker got ponderously to his feet. "You're making it. This is a nice town, mister, and we got along fine before you came. We'll get along fine after you're gone, and that might be sooner than you think."

Lane knew he should turn and walk away. Nothing but trouble would come to him if he stayed. Yet something defiant was stirring in his mind, something that demanded he do what he could to bring whatever this town was hiding into the open, into the light of day. He said deliberately, "I doubt if there's a man in town big enough to make me leave."

Riker's heavy mouth twisted. "I was kind of hoping you'd say that." He moved toward Lane negligently, but in a way that left no doubt what he meant to do.

Behind the man the postmaster spoke up nervously, "Let him alone, Otto. Holt said—"

Riker turned his head. "Shut up," he said savagely. "When I'm through with him he'll crawl if he has to, to get out of town."

Lane backed away slowly, aware that goading Riker had been foolish, yet somehow glad that at last he was going to come to grips with the puzzling hostility he had encountered here. He was also appraising his opponent, assessing his strength and trying to decide what his weaknesses were.

Riker outweighed him by thirty pounds. The strength of the man was obviously tremendous. His chest was broad, deep and heavily muscled, a fact even his loose-fitting shirt failed to hide. His forearms were thick and as heavily muscled. His biceps were tremendous. A solid blow from one of those heavy fists would break Lane's jaw and put him out of the fight for good.

Riker's forehead sloped sharply back from his tiny, deepset eyes. For an instant Lane wondered if he had any weaknesses. None were apparent, certainly.

Riker stalked him ponderously, while Lane backed away. The blacksmith's eyes gleamed with anticipation. He backed Lane against the far wall of the saloon and began to grin. He stepped in close and swung, a short, vicious and well-controlled blow.

Lane ducked under it, coming around, landing his own blow in Riker's belly. All it did was make the big man grunt.

Riker closed with him. The huge hands came out, seized him, picked him up and flung him bodily against the wall. Lane slid down it to the floor, stunned, surprised and suddenly aware that he would be lucky if he managed to avoid being killed.

Riker kicked him savagely. Lane felt his ribs crack and, with pain like a knife in his side, scrambled away before Riker could kick him again. He got to his feet shaking his head, breathing shallowly because of the pain in his ribs.

Riker stalked him again, breathing a bit faster than he had before. He rushed, knocking tables and chairs aside. The bartender yelled, "Hey, take it outside! You'll wreck the place!"

Riker turned his head. "He'll pay for it, Dutch."

Lane knew suddenly that there was only one place he could hurt this man. His body was too heavily muscled to be hurt. Only hard, repeated punches to the jaw would have any effect. He rushed while Riker's head was still turned and landed his blow on the side of Riker's jaw with a sharp and plainly audible crack.

This time, Riker staggered back, a look of pure surprise on his heavy face. Lane followed, and landed a second blow on Riker's jaw before the man could recover himself.

Lane retreated swiftly as Riker charged toward him again. The man's face was red from exertion and shining with sweat. His breath came in short, gusty grunts. His eyes were slightly glazed.

For the first time since the fight had started, Lane felt a touch of hope. Riker had weaknesses—two of them. He was short of breath. He was vulnerable to blows on his jaw. But he could also end the fight in seconds if he got his hands on Lane again.

The table where the gunsmith and postmaster sat was behind Lane now. He saw Riker's eyes go beyond him and saw the way Riker grinned.

Too late, he swung his head. A chair descended on it, smashing, knocking him to his knees. He caught a glimpse of the gunsmith's face, of the man's eyes, bright with savagery.

Riker was on him then. His boot swung, catching him squarely in the chest. And suddenly it was as though there was fire inside of him, red-hot, burning, searing. And he couldn't breathe.

He felt hands raising him. He felt himself held at arm's length with one hand while the other smashed squarely into his face.

Released, he staggered away, to be caught by the gunsmith and knocked back again into Riker's waiting hands.

He could hear harsh laughter as he was knocked from one to the other, and he could hear a wavering, protesting voice, "Riker! Frank! Stop it! You know damn well Holt said to let him alone!"

26

His senses were fading. The feeling of motion increased as he was lifted bodily in Riker's great hands and flung out through the saloon's swinging doors. He fell in the hot dust of the street, groaned and rolled over and at last lay still.

He could hear but he could not move. He heard Riker chuckling and heard him say, "I'll give anybody two to one the bastard takes that stage tomorrow."

There were other voices in the street. One of them, crisp and authoritative, said, "Riker, you're a stupid, bungling fool. Now he'll never leave."

There was silence for a moment and then the same voice said, "Pick him up and take him over to the Vargas house. Saralee will patch him up."

He felt ungentle hands raising him, carrying him along the street. The pain of it was just too much. His consciousness slipped away from him.

CHAPTER 4

When he regained consciousness, he was lying on a sofa, a pillow beneath his head. His face felt puffy. He licked his cracked and broken lips and opened his eyes.

A lamp was shining into them, and he closed them involuntarily. But not before he had seen the face beside the lamp. It was that of the waitress at the hotel.

He opened his eyes again. This time the glare of the lamp was gone and he saw only the face.

There had been fright in it before, but now the fright was gone and anger had taken its place. Her eyes snapped and her face was flushed.

He became conscious of a tightness around his middle and of the fact that his shirt was gone. He glanced down as she said, "You have some cracked ribs—I don't know how many—so I wrapped some strips of cloth around you to hold them in place."

He nodded slightly, his head throbbing fiercely as he did. He winced with the pain.

There were questions he wanted to ask but he didn't ask them. Instead, he looked steadily into her eyes.

Flustered, she said, "I'm Saralee Vargas. That's my father over there."

He turned his head cautiously until he could see across

the room. A man lay on his back on another sofa, mouth open, snoring softly. The girl said bitterly, "He's drunk. He's been drunk ever since . . ." She stopped suddenly.

"Ever since what?"

"Never mind. Do you feel well enough to sit up?"

He nodded carefully. She put her hands beneath his shoulders and helped. He sat up, his head throbbing mercilessly enough to make him close his eyes. Head down, he sat still for several moments, waiting for his senses to stop reeling. Nausea knotted his stomach. Saralee Vargas asked, "Can you make it to the hotel?"

He started to nod his head, then spoke instead. "Sure. If I can get up."

"I'll help you." She helped him rise, steadied him afterward. This close to him, there was a fragrance about her, elusive and faint but very pleasant. Her hands were strong but they were gentle too.

She steered him toward the door, opened it and helped him down the single step off the gallery. She released him. He took a step, staggered and almost fell. She caught him, steadied him again and said reluctantly, "I'll go with you."

Heat was still in the air from the searing day, but there was a breeze, blowing now off the desert and across the river. It helped by drying the sweat on his battered body. He asked, "What time is it? How long . . . ?"

"They brought you here about an hour ago."

They were in the adobe section of town, through which he had passed going to and from the cemetery. It was quiet now, except for the distant strumming of a guitar. He stumbled along the dusty street, wanting to vomit but fighting the compulsion in the presence of this girl. He would be angry tomorrow but tonight he was only very sick.

They reached the hotel. A couple of men on the hotel veranda looked at them curiously, then looked away. They went into the lobby and the girl asked, "Which room do you have?"

"Five."

She helped him up the stairs and along the hall to his door. He fumbled in his pocket for the key, found it and inserted it in the lock. The door opened.

She released him here. He looked at her face in the dim light coming from a single flickering lamp. What he was looking for he could not have said but what he found in her face was the same fright that had been in it when he'd seen her in the hotel dining room. He said shortly, "Thanks," went in and closed the door in her face. He locked it, leaving the key in the lock, then staggered across the room toward the bed. He collapsed on it, face down, and didn't move.

He kept trying to organize his thoughts. The beating had been the first tangible proof of the hostility he had felt since his arrival here. He had not provoked it, unless his refusal to leave town could be considered provocation. But it had been savage and merciless. He didn't know whether he could have outfought Riker or not. He did know he could never beat the man if someone else interfered, as the gunsmith had tonight.

He closed his eyes, but he could not stop his thoughts. And he admitted reluctantly that one thing seemed very sure. Jess was dead. He had died right here in the town of Saguaro. He was buried in one of those unmarked graves.

He found himself thinking of the gunsmith, Frank. Short, stocky and powerful, the man had seemed mild, even meek inside his shop. He had even ducked out the back door and gone after the sheriff to back up his refusal to sell Lane a gun.

He remembered then the way the man's face had looked in the saloon, when he'd caught so brief a glimpse of it. Completely changed. His eyes had been bright with savagery, his mouth twisted with the lust to kill. Unaccountably Lane found himself remembering something else, something all but buried in the distant past. And immediately he saw the connection, knowing why his memory had dredged it up.

He'd been about fifteen at the time. Riding the vast miles of range over which his father's cattle roamed, he'd come on a lone, gaunted cow in a snow-choked ravine. Wolves were pulling at her, leaping in to tear bloody gashes in her shaggy hide, leaping out again when she swung her horned head. There had been a brightness in the eyes of the wolves, an almost obscene lust in their open mouths and lolling tongues. They had looked as the gunsmith had so briefly looked tonight.

He'd shot three of them and the rest had fled. But the cow was dying already. After the wolves had gone, he shot her and left her there.

Had the wolves, the human wolves in Saguaro, pulled Jess down in much the same way? Had they torn him apart for something they thought he had done? And having done so, were they now afraid of having the fact revealed?

It was a shocking thought and it kept him conscious for a while longer as his mind considered it. Then exhaustion and pain took hold of him and he slept.

It was an uneasy and pain-filled sleep. A dozen times he awoke to find that some hurt part of him was cramped, or twisted, and had wakened him. He was glad when morning came, glad even though he could tell it was going to be another scorching day just like the last.

He got stiffly off the bed and staggered to the window

to stare down into the street. He ached in every muscle, it seemed, and his head still throbbed, though not as badly as it had last night.

He crossed to the bureau and dumped water into the wash pan. He soaked the towel in it and mopped gently at his bruised and lacerated face. He stared into the mirror unbelievingly.

His lips were puffy and almost unrecognizable as such. Dried blood was caked on them. One of his eyes was discolored and swelled nearly shut. There were several other bruises and lacerations on his face and the lobe of one ear was torn and swelled.

Below, where his body was not bandaged, bruises were visible, the bruises put there, he supposed, by Riker's boots. It hurt to breathe and it hurt to turn. Carefully, he got another clean shirt out of his carpetbag and with difficulty put in on.

Tucking it in, he discovered that his money belt was gone. Frantically he jammed a hand into his pants pocket and pulled out what change was there. A two-dollar-and-fifty-cent gold piece. A half-dollar. A couple of half-dimes and a few pennies. All the rest was gone.

The gold piece would last him, at most, a couple of days. After that he'd be broke, unable to leave even if he wanted to because he hadn't the stage fare home.

He sat down on the edge of the rumpled bed and stared at the wall of the tiny hotel room. For the briefest moment he felt beaten.

And then, slowly, anger stirred in him. It grew with the passing moments until his face flushed with it, until its stimulus drove away the pain in his battered body and face. God damn this town! They weren't going to defeat him this easily. If they had done what he thought they had he'd see they paid for it. One way or another.

He owed that much to Jess and to his father and brothers back home who had trusted him enough to send him here. He owed it to himself.

Anger made his brain begin to function again. He began to plan what he would do today. Somehow he had to crack the town's secretiveness and hostility.

He'd write and mail a letter home first of all. Then he'd get himself a shovel. He'd walk out to that cemetery at the edge of town and dig up those unmarked graves.

It helped tremendously to have the decision made. He left the room, not bothering to lock it this time, and descended to the desk. He asked the clerk for paper, pencil and an envelope. He was turning away when the man said, "Mr. Sauer."

He turned his head.

"I'm afraid we'll have to ask you to leave today."

"Why?" Lane's voice was clipped with hostility.

The clerk eyed him disapprovingly. "It's . . . well, you know what your face looks like. Our other guests . . . Surely you see how it is."

Lane said flatly, "I'm not going to leave. You can go to hell!" He turned and strode angrily away.

He crossed the lobby to a desk and sat down at it. Frowning, he laboriously wrote his letter asking that several of his brothers be sent to Saguaro to help. He signed his name, put the letter in the envelope and wrote the address on it.

He got up and left the hotel, trying not to limp. He went next door to the post office.

The postmaster was behind the grille. Lane asked, "What's your name, Postmaster?"

"Batterton. Ed Batterton. About last night . . ."

Lane ignored his words. He slid the letter beneath the grille to him. He paid the postage out of his meager store of change. He watched while the postmaster affixed the stamp. Except for one quick glance, the postmaster had refused to meet his eyes. Lane asked, "When will that go out?"

"Today's stage."

Lane nodded and turned away. He went out into the street, blinked painfully a couple of times against the glare, then crossed the street to Holt Childers' mercantile.

No one was in the store but a big, graying, robust-looking man in shirt sleeves, black sleeve protectors and a dark-colored apron. The man had gold-rimmed glasses pinched to his rather impressive-looking nose. He came toward Lane smiling but also managing to look sympathetic and contrite. He put out his hand. "You must be the stranger that came in on the stage yesterday."

"Lane Sauer." He recognized that voice. It was the one he had heard last night as he lay helpless in the street.

"I'm Holt Childers. I'm the mayor of Saguaro. I can't tell you how sorry I am about that business in the saloon last night. I just heard about it a few minutes ago."

Lane stared at him coldly, ignoring the fact that Childers had lied to him. "I want a shovel."

Childers frowned puzzledly. "A shovel? Whatever for?"

"You do sell shovels, don't you?"

"Of course. Come this way." He led Lane toward the rear of the store. Lane found a shovel that would do. He asked, "How much?"

"Fifty cents."

Lane gave him the half-dollar. He said, "This is a damned unfriendly town. What does your sheriff do, just protect the natives here?"

"Oh, you mean your gun." Childers looked regretful. His eyes were blue and the impression they gave of friendliness was conveyed wholly by the lines of affability that surrounded them. The eyes themselves were cold as ice.

"And my money belt. It was lifted off me while I was unconscious from that fight last night."

"Have you reported it to the sheriff?"

Lane shrugged. "Not yet. I doubt if it would be any use anyway. He didn't seem concerned about the gun. I doubt if he'll get very concerned about the money belt."

"I'll talk to him. We can't have this kind of thing happening to visitors who come through here."

"I'm not coming through. I'm here to stay—at least until I find out what happened to my brother Jess. I don't suppose you know anything." He watched Childers carefully as he spoke. There was no sudden altering of the man's expression, no single change he could define. But the change was there. Subtle and almost unnoticeable, it was there.

Childers said, "I'm sorry. I'm afraid . . ."

Lane nodded shortly and turned away. He went out into the street again, put the shovel over his shoulder and headed for the cemetery.

He didn't expect to be allowed to finish the task he had set for himself. He even doubted if he had the strength to dig up two graves. What he did know was that starting to dig them up would stir panic in the town's guilty conscience. He would be stopped, but when he was, he might learn why.

Long before Lane reached the cemetery, he felt light-headed and dizzy. But he kept going stubbornly, trying not to limp or show his pain. He crossed the oven-hot cemetery to the two unmarked graves. Here he rested a moment, leaning on the shovel, staring at the barren, mounded earth.

Anger still burned in him but it was tempered with

sadness now, for he knew Jess was here. Had he not been, there would have been no reason for the treatment he had received at the hands of the townspeople yesterday.

Straightening, he began to dig.

Except for a slight crust on top, the ground was loose. He began to sweat heavily but he found that exertion loosened his bruised muscles.

From time to time he rested, staring back gloomily at the town. He had dug almost two feet before he saw Burt Manus and Holt Childers coming toward him.

Leaning on the shovel, he waited patiently. The pair threaded their way through the headstones and markers. Reaching him, they stopped. Lane stared at the sheriff defiantly.

Manus was frowning. He said harshly, "Who told you you could come out here and dig up this grave? What the hell's the matter with you anyway?"

"I'm trying to find out who's buried here."

"I can tell you that. You don't have to dig it up. One of 'em was a drifter that shot it out with a couple of cowboys several months ago. Reason there's no marker is that nobody knew his name."

"What about the other one?"

"What the hell is this, anyway? These men are dead. If one of 'em was your brother, do you think I'd try and keep it from you?"

"Then you should have no objection to me diggin' 'em up. Who's it going to hurt?"

"It's against the law. Now get up out of that grave and go on back to town. And be on the stage this afternoon."

"I can't be. Somebody lifted my money belt while I was unconscious after the fight last night. I haven't got the fare."

36

Childers spoke for the first time, after clearing his throat uneasily. "We'll see that you get the fare."

Lane stared at him sourly. "Whose pocket will it come out of, Mayor? Yours or the sheriff's? Or will the blacksmith dig it up?"

Manus said, "That's enough of that kind of talk. Are you going to leave or do I have to put another lump on your head?"

Lane raised the shovel. "Try it, Sheriff. Let's just get this settled now."

The sheriff shifted his weight slightly. Holt Childers said, "Stop it, Burt. We don't want any more . . ." He stopped, looking helplessly from the sheriff to Lane and back again.

Lane asked, "Any more of what? What is it you don't want any more of, Mr. Mayor? Killin' strangers? You told me who was in one of these graves. Who's in the other one?"

Burt Manus turned his head and stared truculently at Childers. When he looked at Lane again, there was grim determination in his eyes. He said softly, "I'll tell you just once more. Fill in that grave and go back to town or I'll put you under arrest. Resist arrest and I'll shoot you. Is that clear?"

Lane nodded. He could see the sheriff meant exactly what he said. He stepped up out of the grave and began to fill it in. He glanced up at the two men once, thinking that, if he wanted to, he could throw dirt in their faces and overpower them.

He also realized that if he did he would be finished here. The sheriff could jail him and he might rot there for all anybody would care. The way this town was run he could be railroaded or killed and nobody would give a damn.

He finished filling in the grave, sweating heavily. He leaned on the handle and panted. "You're hiding something. You're all hiding something and I'm going to find out what it is."

Neither man replied immediately but there was a firming in both their expressions that told Lane something had been decided by the statement he had just made. The sheriff said almost wearily, "Get on the stage when it comes in, Sauer. Your fare will be paid to wherever you came from. If you don't . . . well, hell, I'm not going to be responsible."

Lane said, "I may go, but I'll be back. I've got five brothers at home. We'll all be coming back."

He knew immediately that he should have kept still. The threat had been a mistake. He was alone here, in an openly hostile town. He knew suddenly that he wasn't likely to have a chance to get on the stage. Not now.

Manus and Childers turned heavily and walked away, side by side. Neither spoke to the other. Neither turned his head. They disappeared into the winding, narrow streets of the adobe, Mexican section of the town.

Lane stared at the two graves for several moments before he followed them. When he did, he carried the shovel over his shoulder. It wasn't much of a weapon but it was better than nothing. For now at least. He had the feeling that if he wanted to stay alive another night he'd better get himself a gun.

He was scared but he was mad too. He was mad clear through. This town had murdered Jess and buried him in an unmarked grave. Lane meant to find out why.

He walked along the narrow, dusty street. Halfway to the center of town he stopped. A man had come out of one of the adobe houses, a man whose eyes were red, whose unshaven face was blotched, a man he recognized as the drunk Saralee Vargas had pointed out to him as her father the night before.

He stopped. The man stared at him, shuddered visibly and then looked away as though he had seen a ghost. Lane stopped. He said, "You're Mr. Vargas, aren't you?"

The man nodded but he did not look up. He was a short man, partly bald and dark of skin. He tried to push past Lane but Lane blocked the way. Vargas peered up. "Please, *señor*. I am sick. I need a drink."

Lane said, "Maybe you can tell me. About my brother."

"No, *señor*. I know nothing of your brother. Let me go, *señor*. I am sick. I need a drink."

"Why do you need a drink? Is there something you're trying to forget?" Lane's voice was cold with anger.

Vargas began to shake. Lane seized his shirt front. He forced the man to look at him. "Damn you, I want the truth! This town killed him, didn't it? Everybody in town had a part in it, didn't they?"

Vargas' face had turned a pasty gray. "*Señor* . . ." He nodded suddenly. "*Sí, señor*. They killed him. He is buried there . . ." He gestured vaguely toward the cemetery.

"Why did they kill him? Why?" There was sickness in Lane now, sickness that had nothing to do with the beating he'd taken last night.

"They thought . . . that he had killed a woman."

"But he hadn't? Is that it?"

The man nodded numbly. "Afterward . . . the next day . . . that other one . . ." He gestured again vaguely toward the cemetery. "That other one shot it out with Nicolo Finch and another man. Before he died he said it was he who killed the woman. But it was too late, *señor*. It was too late." He shuddered again.

"How did they kill him?" He knew the answer, he thought, but he had to be sure.

"They hanged him, *señor*."

Lane's stomach knotted. He thought he would vomit as his mind created a picture of Jess dangling from a scaffold. . . . He said harshly, "And you. You helped too, didn't you?"

Vargas was shaking uncontrollably. He began to weep, brokenly like a child. Lane stood aside and watched the man stumble and weave along the dusty street toward town.

He stood there numbly for a long, long time. He knew what he had come to find out. He knew what they were hiding and why they were hostile to him. And he knew something else. They would not now let him leave. They would kill him to protect their secret, to keep hidden their awful shame.

Ed Batterton stared for a long, long time at the letter Lane Sauer had handed him. Then he crammed it into his pocket and came out from behind the grille. He went out the door, locking it behind him, and scurried across the street to Holt Childers' mercantile.

He went inside, but stopped abruptly when he saw Sauer at the rear of the store with Holt. He ducked down behind a counter as Lane came toward the front of the store, carrying a new shovel he had bought. Sauer went out and Batterton stood up. He stared into the worried face of Childers and asked almost breathlessly, "What's he going to do with that?"

Childers scowled at him. "Dig, I suppose. What does a man usually do with a shovel?" He glared at Batterton briefly. "What the hell are you doing here?"

Batterton dragged the letter out of his pocket. He handed it to Holt.

Childers read the name and address on the envelope.

He ripped the envelope open, unfolded and read the letter. He wadded up both envelope and letter in his big, powerful hand. "Go on, Ed. Get out of here. If he asks, tell him the letter is with the rest of the mail and will go out on today's stage."

Batterton started to go, then whirled around. "What are we going to do?"

"We'll sit tight and keep our mouths shut until we get rid of him."

"What do you mean, get rid of him?"

"Oh, for Christ's sake! What I meant was that Burt is going to make him take the stage and get out of town."

"He'll go home. He'll get help and come back. And then what're we going to do?"

"We'll let Burt handle it. Now go on back to work. And keep your mouth shut, understand?"

Batterton nodded dumbly, turned, and hurried out of the store. At the door, he glanced up and down the street, then hurried across. He went into the post office and slammed the door behind him.

He didn't know what had been in the letter, but he could guess. Sauer had written home for help.

He tried to work, but had to give it up. His hands were shaking so violently that he couldn't do anything. He began to pace back and forth nervously.

He closed his eyes, holding them tightly shut only long enough to see again the picture that had tormented him every night for months, the tight-stretched rope with its bulky hangman's knot forcing the head to one side, the congested face, the bulging eyes, the tongue lolling out, the drool of saliva coming from one corner of the dying man's open mouth.

Panic touched his thoughts. Was he losing his mind?

Was he going insane? He hadn't had a decent night's sleep in months. In God's name, why couldn't he forget?

No wonder Severo Vargas had gone back to the bottle. No wonder tempers in Saguaro were touchy. If the thing tormented everyone the way it tormented him, no wonder everybody was on edge.

He thought of Lane Sauer, of the man's stubborn obstinacy. If he stayed in town another day he'd know. He'd know what had happened and then . . .

And then what? What could he do? He couldn't exact revenge against every man who had participated in the lynching of Jess Sauer because that included every man in town and several who lived outside of it.

One thing was certain, though. If the story got out, Saguaro had better forget about its ambitions to be more than it was right now. A blot like this would make a ghost town out of it. It would ruin every inhabitant living here.

But Childers had said Burt Manus would handle it. All right, let him handle it. He was the sheriff. He had given Sauer to the mob rather than shoot into them. The responsibility was his. Let him shoulder it.

CHAPTER 5

Walking away from Lane Sauer at the cemetery, Burt
Manus scowled savagely. Sauer was a stubborn one. He
wouldn't leave of his own free will. He'd have to be put
on that stage in irons. Somebody would have to go with
him to see that he did not get off. Nor would getting him
out of town solve the problem permanently. He'd come
back, bringing his brothers along with him, and then the
problem would be bigger and less solvable than it was
right now.

So deeply was he involved with his own thoughts that
Holt Childers' voice immediately beside him made him
start. Childers said, "We'll have to get rid of him, Burt.
It's the only way."

He turned his ponderous head and stared at Holt. The
man's face was pale and his eyes looked scared. Manus
asked sarcastically, "And how the hell do you propose to
do that? Do you want to kill him or do you want me to?"

"You could . . . you've told him to leave town and
you know damned well he won't. Why don't you recover
his gun and money belt and give them back to him?
Maynard Brooks has got his gun. Riker's probably got
his money belt. Then order him to get on the stage. If
he pulls his gun you'll be justified in killing him."

"That'd be the easy way out for you, wouldn't it, Holt? It'd be easy for all the rest of them too, letting me do their goddam dirty work." He stared at Childers, unconcealed hatred in his eyes. And yet, not all the hatred was directed at the mayor. A good part of it was for himself. He could have defended his prisoner when they came after him only he'd convinced himself that a woman-killer wasn't worth the risk of shooting into the massed townsmen outside the jail. He'd prejudged Sauer and found him guilty of killing Lorina Newkirk. He'd let them have him because he wasn't willing to kill or wound any of them in his defense.

Holt Childers said, "Think, Burt, think. If it gets out, this town is finished. We're all finished. Saguaro will be a ghost town in a year."

The sheriff nodded. Childers was right about that. It was one thing to have secret guilt eating at your insides day after day but you could learn to live with it because everyone you saw was equally guilty and because you knew not one of them would ever speak of it. But if the whole world knew . . . if the papers all over the territory carried the story . . . hell, the men of this town would be like that man-eater up in the San Juan Mountains of Colorado—forever branded, forever outcast. Even if nobody was tried. Even if nobody went to jail.

If he let Lane Sauer leave . . . Sauer would bring his brothers back with him and the story would come out. Someone would break. Someone would talk.

He thought back over the years, over his years of keeping the peace. He'd started out with the Rangers, down in Texas. After the war he'd drifted west and had wound up here when half a sheriff's time was still spent chasing bands of renegade Apaches. Until six months ago he'd

44

worn his star with pride. Until six months ago he'd never done a thing of which he was ashamed.

He wondered briefly what Mary would have said about the Sauer business if she had been alive, but he didn't have to wonder long. He knew what she would have said, or what she would have thought, even if she'd kept it to herself. He was glad she hadn't lived to see him give his prisoner to a mob. He was glad, at least, that she hadn't had to share his shame.

Such a fine line had been between giving Sauer to the mob and defending him. He had almost, damn it, he had almost fired that shotgun he'd had in his hands that night. If he hadn't been so sure Sauer was guilty. If he hadn't been so sure. . . .

He and Childers reached River Street, on which the town's businesses were located. Childers turned uptown toward his store. Manus crossed and went into the hotel.

Maynard Brooks was at the desk. Manus put both big hands flat on its top. He said softly, "I'll take his gun and belt, Maynard."

Brooks began to sputter, but stopped under the steady impact of the sheriff's eyes. He reached under the desk and withdrew the gun and belt. He laid it on the desk resentfully.

Manus picked it up, wound the belt around the holster and carried it outside.

The sun was already blistering but Manus had been here so long he didn't really notice it. He was like a desert lizard in that he could absorb the heat without any real discomfort. He paused for a moment, wondering if by recovering Sauer's gun and money belt he was not unconsciously accepting Childers' solution for eliminating the man. Shaking his head impatiently, he headed for the jail.

45

The door was not locked. He went in and laid the gun and belt on the desk. Then he went out again and walked past the row of cribs to the livery barn.

Riker had the forge going and was working the bellows with a foot while he heated a horseshoe. A horse stood tied nearby.

Manus noted with some satisfaction that Riker's face was marked almost as badly as Sauer's was. He looked at the man distastefully. Riker was a type he could not abide, a bully, a man with little intelligence who made up for it by beating men of lesser physical strength. He said coldly, "Give me his money belt, Riker. With everything intact."

"I haven't got it. What the hell's the matter with you, coming in here and accusing me . . . ?"

Manus said evenly, "Damn you, Riker, I didn't come here to argue with you! Go get it."

Riker tried to stare him down, but in the end his eyes shifted and fell away. He began to curse, softly and beneath his breath. He turned and shuffled back into the barn. He fumbled beneath some grain sacks and returned carrying the money belt. Manus took it without a word. He started to leave, then turned. "Everything's here, isn't it? If you lie to me and I find out, I'll throw you in the jug."

"It's all there, you damn—"

"Easy, Riker!"

"What are you getting so high and mighty for? You're as guilty as any of us are. You let us have him. You could have stopped it but you let us have him. You never even put up a fight."

Manus turned on his heel and went out into the sun. He felt dirty, soiled. But he felt cornered, too. And desperate. Was a whole lifetime of honest, efficient law enforcement going to go down the drain because of a single split-second error of judgment? What was a man supposed

46

to do, anyway, fire a double-barreled ten-gauge into a crowd of people he'd known and respected for a good part of his life? He knew the answer before his mind even asked the question. It was yes. He was sworn to uphold the law and a mob bent on murder was still a mob bent on murder no matter how respectable its members were in their everyday lives.

Respectable! His mouth curled with contempt. They'd been slavering like a bunch of wolves when they took Jess Sauer out and hanged him. But afterward—not a damned one of them had either the guts or decency to cut him down and bury him. That had been Manus' job. He turned his head and stared at the foliage of Saguaro's lone cottonwood tree showing above the feed store across the street. He shuddered slightly as though with a sudden chill.

He walked back to the sheriff's office. As he reached it, he saw Lane Sauer crossing River Street toward the hotel, the shovel over his shoulder. He yelled, "Sauer!"

The man turned his head and Manus beckoned him. He went into the office and waited nervously. He had just made up his mind what he was going to do. He knew it was fraught with risk, but he also knew it was the right thing to do. He was going to give Sauer back his gun and money belt. He was going to stop trying to get Sauer to leave town. He was going to go on doing his job and if that meant protecting Sauer from the town, then that was the way it would have to be.

He'd made a mistake in judgment the night Sauer's brother was lynched. He wasn't going to compound that mistake with a whole series designed to conceal the first.

The decision would probably destroy him. It might even kill him in the end, but he was glad that it was made. He waited and when Sauer stepped through the door, handed him the gun and money belt. He said, "Count the money, Mr. Sauer. I want to know if it's all there."

Sauer put down his shovel, took the belt and strapped it around his middle. He buckled on the gunbelt, withdrew the gun and checked its loads. Manus repeated, "Check the money in that belt. I want to know if it's all there."

Sauer looked at him, a disconcerting quality about his steady stare. He unbuckled the money belt and checked its contents. He nodded. "It's all there."

Manus asked, trying to keep a hopeful quality out of his voice, "Are you leaving on the stage?"

"No. I know what happened to my brother Jess. But I still don't know why. I think that before I leave I want to know the whole dirty story. I owe him that much."

"How . . . who . . . ?"

"Vargas. The drunk."

Manus opened his mouth to speak, then scowled and shut it again. Any explanation would sound weak. He said, "Suppose I told you the whole story? Would you leave?"

Sauer shook his head. There was both anger and contempt in his eyes, but he did not speak.

"Why? Is it revenge you want?"

"Maybe. I don't know. All I can think about is Jess, choking, his face turning red, then blue. All I can think about is the people of this town, doing that to him for something he hadn't even done."

"They'll kill you, Sauer. They'll kill you the way they killed him."

Sauer just stared at him. Manus sat down heavily at the desk. He wanted to justify himself. He said, "I had a choice to make. I had to fire into them or let them come in and take my prisoner. I hesitated. God damn it, man, that's all I did. I hesitated and then it was too late."

Still Sauer didn't say anything. At last he turned and went out into the street, leaving the shovel behind. He walked uptown in the direction of the hotel, disappearing from Burt Manus' sight.

A grimace like one caused by real physical pain crossed the sheriff's face. The man was a fool, he thought. The man was a stupid fool. This town would eat him alive. What Riker had done to him last night was mild compared to what they'd do to him if he stayed.

His expression settled gloomily. He'd made a mistake that night. Now it was time to pay for it.

CHAPTER 6

Severo Vargas shambled blindly along the dusty street until he reached River Street. He was sweating heavily, not a normal sweat caused by the heat but a clammy one caused by fear and self-disgust. Tremors in his legs made it difficult for him to walk.

He needed a drink. Oh God, he needed a drink. He stumbled toward Dutch's saloon, then hurried past when he saw several men inside. He went beyond to Newkirk's place, which was called the Emporia.

Jake Newkirk scowled at him as he came in. The place was empty. It had been empty for months. Vargas didn't know how Jake held on.

Jake had been drinking too. His face was flushed and his eyes had a vague, mean look to them. Vargas crossed to the bar and said, "Whisky, Jake."

Severo was second-generation Mexican. He had been born in an adobe shack in the mountains east of town, twenty miles away. His parents had spoken nothing but Spanish but Severo spoke both Spanish and English with equal fluency. Sometimes he mixed the two languages but it was from habit rather than necessity.

Jake shoved a bottle and glass at him and Severo laid a coin on the bar. With trembling hands he poured a drink and gulped it down. He gagged, recovered and poured another one. Jake had given him the worst whisky in the place but he didn't care. As long as he got it down.

Jake poured another for himself. He scowled at Vargas silently. Vargas raised his second drink with a hand a bit steadier than before. He gulped it, afterward glancing obliquely at Newkirk behind the bar.

There was a reason the Emporia was empty nowadays. The reason went back six months. Newkirk's wife was the woman who had been killed, and Newkirk had led the mob. The town blamed him for it, believing that without him there would have been no mob. Only they were wrong. Severo knew that, if they did not. If Jake hadn't led them, someone else would have. There had been a will to murder in Saguaro that awful night.

Vargas stared bleakly at the bottle and glass before him, the streaks of tears still visible on his face. He remembered his own part in it.

After the death of his wife, three years ago, he'd begun to drink. He had discovered that sometimes, if he got drunk enough, she would appear to him in his thoughts and occasionally in his dreams. But as the months went on, she came to him less frequently until she stopped returning altogether, no matter whether he was sober or whether he was drunk.

He probably could have quit right then except that the habit of drink was strong. So he went on, drinking to forget the fact that he could no longer even remember Juana's face.

A year before the lynching, he had quit. Saralee made him quit. She told him bluntly one day that if he did not quit she intended to leave home and go to Santa Fe.

A year, he was, without a drink of any kind. Not even beer. And then came that terrible night, while the mob formed, while Burt Manus stood his solitary vigil down at the jail.

Passions had been high. He remembered Holt Childers shouting from the bar in the Emporia—right here—that this had to be a united thing. The whole town had to participate—every man in it. One of their women had been attacked and killed. Retribution, swift and terrible, coming from every single man in town, would serve notice, he said, to every potential woman-killer that Saguaro would not tolerate them. He remembered trying to slip away unseen, remembered their scorn and their accusations of cowardice. What if it had been Saralee, they asked, lying stripped and bloody on the dusty ground.

So he'd gone with them. To his everlasting shame, he'd gone with them. He'd stood in their ranks while they faced the sheriff and his gun. He'd helped drag Sauer out, down the street to the lone cottonwood tree behind the feed store on the riverbank. He'd shut his ears to the man's protestations of innocence and had, himself, shouted during the short, mock trial, "How did you get those scratches then?"

When Sauer screamed that he'd gotten them riding through brush, Severo had not believed. But when he saw the man sitting on his horse with a noose around his neck—he had been sorry then. He had almost cried out at them to stop.

Almost. But he had not cried out. He had watched as the whip fell, as the horse lunged ahead leaving the grisly thing hanging there, swinging like a pendulum, back and forth, back and forth. . . .

Severo shuddered and poured himself another drink. He remembered walking back up River Street afterward, trying to forget the sounds the man made as he had choked to death. He still heard those sounds, still saw that ghastly human pendulum in his dreams.

They'd been subdued, those men, but grim and righteous afterward. They'd all trooped up to the Emporia saloon, some of them spilling over to fill Dutch's place. They'd had their drinks, telling each other that it was a terrible thing but that it'd had to be done. And Severo, because he knew it was not necessary, because he knew in his heart that it was murder and that he had taken part, began that night to drink again.

Not until the next day did the recriminations begin. Nicolo Finch and another man, riding the desert for cattle, came upon a stranger who, without reason, shot at them. They split and came up on two sides of him, and between them, fatally wounded him. Dying, he told them he had killed Jake Newkirk's wife. He had begged for a priest so that he could confess his sin and be absolved of guilt.

Nicolo Finch brought the body, and with it the news, into town. For twenty-four hours, Saguaro was silent as a tomb. No one would look at anyone else. Wives did not speak to their husbands or husbands to their wives. At last, because each man sought desperately to absolve himself, they began to point fingers at those who had started it. At Jake Newkirk. At Holt Childers. At Burt Manus, because he hadn't stopped it when he could, because he hadn't done his job and held his prisoner. It would have been better, they said that day, if he had shot into them. He would have stopped them from becoming murderers.

The recriminations lasted for a week. After that, Holt Childers called them together and told them that the lynching had to be kept secret or the town would be ruined and that each man in it would share the ruin of the town. Saguaro was already the county seat, he said, and had a good chance of becoming the territorial capital.

Some day, the territory would be a state, and Saguaro, located as it was on the riverbank, could become its capital.

For six months now, the town had kept its secret and no man had spoken of the lynching. But each had lived with his own personal sense of guilt. Each had known, if no other did, what his own responsibility for the tragedy was.

Now the secret was out. Sauer's brother had come to town. He had caught Severo Vargas a few minutes before, sick and desperately needing his morning drink, and had forced the truth out of him.

He glanced guiltily at Jake. He fumbled for another coin, laid it on the bar and hurried out. If they knew he'd talked . . . He began to shiver in spite of the heat.

In near panic, he glanced up and down the street. He saw Sauer come out of the sheriff's office, wearing a gun belted around his waist. He turned and ran between the two saloons to the alley and beyond.

He fell half a dozen times. Each time, sobbing with terror and shortness of breath, he got up and ran again. He did not stop until he had reached his house, until he had gone in, slammed and barred the door. He sat down on a straight-backed chair, shaking with exhaustion and fear. He stared emptily at the floor between his feet.

The weight of the gun was a comforting thing to Lane as he walked toward the hotel. They might kill him, but he would not die helplessly.

He understood the hostility he had felt within this town now. He had imagined nothing; it had been here, tangible and real from the moment he had walked into the hotel.

He was, in this moment, too stunned to be angry, too confused to be thinking of revenge. He was thinking of Jess, alone, set upon by an enraged town and accused of something he hadn't done. He was thinking of his brother, dragged from the jail in the dead of night by a slavering, drunken mob and hanged without being given an opportunity to defend himself. He was thinking of the sheriff, too, who had faced the mob with a gun he would not use, who had stood aside and let them come into his jail and take his prisoner away from him.

And he was thinking that the men of this town had not changed. Their guilt was not entirely for the awful thing they had done. Whatever pity they might feel was not for Jess, who had died uselessly and wrongfully but for themselves. Furthermore, they were prepared to kill again to protect their secret from the world. They would kill him if they could, in whatever way they could. Each would, of course, prefer that someone else do the dirty job. But it would be done.

He reached the hotel and paused for a moment, staring at the post office next door. His letter would not go out on the stage today. He knew that as surely as he had ever known anything. It had probably already been destroyed. But there was a way. . . .

He went into the hotel lobby. He crossed to the desk. The clerk glanced at him uneasily, saying nothing of his earlier demand that Lane check out of the hotel. Lane asked for paper and an envelope. The clerk pushed it across the desk to him silently. Lane turned and went up the stairs.

He went into his room, sat down and wrote his letter carefully. He put it in the envelope, sealed it and addressed the envelope. If he could get it to the stage driver and pay him to mail it somewhere east of here, there was a chance the letter might get through.

He put the envelope in his pocket immediately, seeing the faultiness of his reasoning. He would be watched every minute he was in the street. If he passed a letter to the stage driver he would be seen doing it. Someone would ride out and overtake the stage. They'd get the letter back.

But if he could ride out and intercept the stage . . . He shook his head gloomily. Riker ran the livery barn. Riker wouldn't rent him a horse.

He needed help. He'd never get the letter out by himself. But who would help? Who in this guilty town would help?

Shrugging with discouragement, he got up and left his room. He descended to the lobby and headed for the dining room. It seemed indecent for him to be hungry but he was. All day yesterday he'd eaten only that free lunch in the saloon. He'd had nothing yet today.

There was no one in the dining room, no one but the girl Saralee. He sat down and she crossed the room to him. "How do you feel today?"

He nodded unsmilingly. "Better. Have you got some soup?"

She nodded and hurried toward the kitchen. At least, he thought, they weren't going to try to starve him to death. There had still been fear in her eyes this morning, but there had been something else as well, something that had not been in them yesterday. He decided it was a combination of pity and anger. Pity for him because of what she knew he faced—anger because of the injustice of his having to face it at all.

She returned, carrying a tray on which there was a steaming bowl of soup. As she put it down in front of him he said softly, "I know what happened here six months ago. I know my brother was hanged."

She started so violently that she almost spilled the soup. He said, "They won't let me get out of town alive. If

56

I try to leave, someone will kill me. You know that's true, don't you?"

She gave no sign that she had heard. He said in an urgent whisper, "I've got to get a letter out. I'll leave it under my plate when I'm finished with the soup. If you could get it to the stage driver, or that whisky drummer that came in yesterday . . ."

Her face was white as she straightened and walked away. She did not look at him.

He began to eat, a difficult and painful process because of his smashed and swollen lips. After taking several spoonfuls of soup, he raised his head and casually looked around. There was no one in the doorway leading from the dining room to the lobby. There was no one at the windows looking in from the street. But he knew he had been watched while the girl was serving him. He knew that certainly, and wondered if he had been seen talking to her. He'd tried to keep his voice low. He'd tried to talk without looking up at her. It was possible no one had realized.

And yet, he thought, why should she help? Her own father had been part of the mob.

He finished the soup, finished also the bread she had brought with it. He felt stronger than he had before, and with his returning strength came tension that was almost unbearable. Death would stalk him from this moment on. But he had to stay alive. He *had* to. Jess deserved something better than to lie nameless in that barren stretch of desert next to a rapist and a murderer. Nor should those who had murdered him go unpunished and unknown.

He fumbled for his pipe and tobacco. He withdrew the letter from his pocket along with his tobacco pouch. The letter was under the pouch when he laid it down beside his plate.

He dropped the pipe awkwardly. When he picked it up, he shoved the letter beneath the plate.

With trembling fingers, he filled the pipe and lighted it. The girl returned and he paid her for the meal. Her eyes were terrified.

He got up and left the dining room. He walked through the lobby and out into the street. He stopped there, smoking, feeling his own unbearable tension and feeling too the unseen eyes that were watching him. He didn't know what to do. He didn't know what he should do next. He supposed he could only wait until Saguaro's guilt took the initiative.

CHAPTER 7

Across from the hotel, Judge Tom Kemmerer sat in his swivel chair before the window, staring down into the street. He saw Lane Sauer, a gun belted around his waist, come into view and go into the hotel.

He'd had several visitors already this morning. It did not surprise him when Harris Gentry knocked on his door and entered. He glanced around.

Gentry, the county attorney, was a big, imposing man in his mid-fifties. He had been a colonel in the Confederate Army during the war, and had been decorated by Jeff Davis himself. He talked with a soft Tennessee drawl, but there were times when that drawl took on the ring of naked steel. Staring at him now, Kemmerer wondered how either he or Gentry could have been drawn into that affair six months ago. What madness had possessed them both? Everything in the training both of them had received, everything they stood for forbade participation in a lynching. And that was exactly what it had been, despite the mock trial over which he had presided. Jess Sauer had never had a chance.

Today, Gentry's normally overpowering self-confidence seemed shaken. He was frowning worriedly and he looked

59

a little pale. He said, "He knows, Judge. Now we're going to have to decide what to do with him."

Kemmerer stared at Gentry. He remembered that Gentry had been seeing Lorina Newkirk before the tragedy. He'd seen him once himself, slipping into her house after dark. He also knew that Gentry was not the only one.

His stare took on an abstract quality as he wondered what it was the woman had possessed, what quality, that made her lovers willing to close their eyes to an obvious truth and fall so deeply in love with her. And for the first time he realized it was this quality in Lorina that had made the lynching possible.

Gentry said, with a touch of impatience in his voice, "I said we were going to have to decide what to do with him."

Kemmerer tore his thoughts away from Lorina with the rueful realization that even he, for all his sixty years, had wanted her. He hadn't been able to help himself. She had a way of looking at a man . . .

He said, "There's not much choice, is there? We either let him go or see to it that he doesn't go. One way he ruins us. The other, he makes murderers out of us a second time."

Even as he spoke, he was thinking that if Lorina's tastes in men had run to those like her husband and Riker down at the livery barn, Jess Sauer would still have been alive. But she had liked cultured men. Men with clean hands and shirts. Which meant the prominent men in the town, the town's leaders. Its judge, its mayor, its county attorney, its businessmen. Only these men could have wielded the influence that had made one hundred per cent participation in the lynching possible. Only these men could have kept Burt Manus from firing his shotgun into the mob.

Gentry said, "Damn it, Tom, we made a mistake. Nobody denies that. But we thought we were doing right. We're not murderers."

Kemmerer's eyes narrowed slightly. "Aren't we? Search your soul honestly for a change, Harris. Why were you so enraged when you saw Lorina's body on the slab downstairs? Was your outrage for the sanctity of womanhood that had been violated? Or was your grief personal?"

"Damn you, Judge, I don't have to stand here and take that from you."

"I'm sorry, Harris. I suppose I had no right. My hands are as dirty as yours. But I know one thing. They're not going to get any dirtier. If this town wants to kill that man they'll have to do it without me."

"I didn't say we had to kill him. Stop putting words into my mouth."

Kemmerer looked at him steadily. "What *did* you mean, Harris?"

Gentry's face flushed angrily. He uttered a short obscenity. Shaking with rage, he turned toward the door. Halfway there, he turned and came back, mastering his anger with an obvious effort. He said, "If we don't pull together, Tom, we're lost. This isn't my problem. Neither is it yours. It's the problem of every man in town."

Kemmerer said softly, "But one each man must solve for himself. I don't know what I *will* do yet, but I do know what I won't do. I won't have a part in that man's death. I'll prevent it if I can."

Gentry stared at him furiously for several moments. Then he turned and stalked from the room. The door slammed thunderously.

Kemmerer leaned back in his chair and closed his eyes. He was a lonely man; he had been a lonely man since Lucy had died eighteen years ago. He'd been only forty-two when Lucy died. He'd traveled to Tucson, Santa Fe, Albuquerque and once as far as Chicago but he'd never found a woman in any of those places with whom he could fall in love. But he was sure, in spite of what he knew of her, that he could have fallen in love with Lorina Newkirk. He could have fallen as deeply in love with her as Gentry had, as had Holt Childers and Maynard Brooks.

He had searched his own soul in the last six months, as honestly as he knew how. He had admitted that his own fury at seeing Lorina's ravaged body had been personal. He had wanted her. In a lonely old man's way he had hoped that one day she would turn to him.

And so, when Jess Sauer had been arrested with scratches on his face, he had allowed himself to be drawn into the madness, the hysteria that swept the town.

Now his career was at an end. He would resign his post as county judge. Someway, somehow, he would try to find a way to forgive himself.

An expression of distaste touched his face as he recognized his own hypocrisy. He was sixty and he knew the future held little for him in the way of personal advancement, power or position. There wasn't time for it. He could afford to take a noble stand, to tell Gentry that he would not compound his crime by participating in Sauer's death. He had little or nothing to lose. The scorn that would be heaped on him by the world once the crime of Saguaro was known would be nothing to the scorn he had heaped on himself in the last six months, or the self-contempt with which he would live all the rest of his life.

But how about the others? Gentry was young enough to be prominent in the new state that would be formed out of this territory some day. Holt Childers was young enough to one day become a millionaire. The others had wives and children to think about. He had only himself.

His expression changed to one of anguish. That unwelcome vision came to him again, the black sky, the torches, the green foliage of the town's lone cottonwood.

And the long, horizontal branch, stout enough to stand the jerk of a body yanked off the back of a startled horse. The body itself, swaying back and forth like some obscene pendulum . . .

A shudder shook him and he felt nausea crawling in his stomach just as he had that night. He'd sentenced a lot of men to death in his years as judge. But until six months ago he'd done it lawfully, in good conscience, and had never let his personal feelings intervene.

Why, he thought in agony, hadn't they waited one day more? If they had, Jess Sauer would still be alive. The men of Saguaro would not be faced with the terrible decision they had to make today.

It seemed like a long, long time before he saw Sauer come out of the hotel. Sauer stood on the veranda before the door and deliberately relighted his pipe.

Judge Kemmerer held his breath, half expecting a rifle shot to ring out in the quiet street.

Sauer looked like a rock standing there, legs spread, pipe gripped between his strong white teeth. He looked unkillable.

It was an illusion. He was mortal like anybody else. It would only take a tiny piece of lead to change that tough and vital man into a lump of dead flesh.

Kemmerer's eyes narrowed as he studied Sauer's face. It was a strong face, showing none of the doubt and uncertainty that must be in his mind. It looked as though it had been hewn out of stone and never quite finished or polished. Something close to a smile touched the judge's mouth. Lane Sauer was a tough adversary, even for this guilty town. Standing there on the hotel veranda, Sauer looked as though he was, even now, throwing out a challenge to the town.

The whisky drummer came out of the Uptown Saloon and scurried across the street to the hotel. Reaching it, he shoved his hat back on his head, drew out the same soiled handkerchief and mopped his streaming brow. He looked at Lane, on the point of uttering some ill-tempered complaint about the weather, then stopped himself. He said, "Whew! What happened to you?"

Lane put up a hand and ruefully touched his face. He grinned, feeling his swollen, bruised lips stretch and crack. "Nothin' that won't heal, I guess." He waited a moment, then asked, "You leaving Saguaro soon?"

"Noon stage. I got my business done. Next stop's in the high country north of here, thank God." His voice was high, thin, without much body to it. Lane watched him go into the hotel, hoping Saralee Vargas wouldn't act too terrified when she gave the letter to him. If the drummer thought he was taking any chance . . . if he thought there was any risk, then he'd just refuse to have anything to do with it.

He walked over and sat down in one of the wooden rockers. It squeaked slightly as he rocked. There was shade here but the heat was almost as bad as it was out in the sun. He began to sweat.

He wondered what would happen if he just walked out when the stage came in at noon and got aboard. Surely they wouldn't dare stop him in front of witnesses. They'd have to let him go.

It was worth a try, he thought. He didn't think he'd make it, but anything that would needle the town was worth trying.

64

He got up suddenly and crossed the street. He went into the furniture store directly across from the hotel.

It was cooler here, perhaps because of the second story, which insulated it from the direct rays of the sun. One side of the store had furniture in it, the other hardware. The two sides were divided by a wide aisle leading toward the rear where there was a long counter.

Lane walked slowly to the counter. A man sitting at a desk looked up.

This was a man in his early forties, Lane judged. He had iron gray hair and a strong, determined face. There seemed to be both anger and resentment in him as he asked, "Something I can do for you?"

Lane said, "I want to buy a grave marker. How soon can you have it ready for me?"

The man flinched. He got up, a wiry, powerful man about the same size as Lane. His hands were calloused and brown, the hands of a carpenter. He reached for a pad of paper and pencil and shoved them across the counter to Lane. "Write the name and date."

"I know the name but not the date. Maybe you could fill that in."

The man licked his lips. He started to speak, then changed his mind. Lane wrote, "Jess Sauer. Murdered, . . ." He shoved the paper back to the man. "How much will that be?"

The man looked at the paper. His hands began to shake and he clenched them angrily. "Two-fifty, I guess."

"Can you have it today?"

The man nodded. Lane put down a two-fifty gold piece. He said, "I'm his brother, Lane."

The man glanced up. He looked like he wanted to run but he looked like he wanted to kill Lane too. He mumbled, "Harry Zeeb."

65

Lane turned and walked back to the front of the store. He knew he'd never get the grave marker. He also knew as soon as he went out the front door Harry Zeeb would go out the back. He'd go to somebody, probably to Holt Childers who seemed to run the town.

He went out, then on impulse turned the corner and walked along the side street to the alley. He heard a door open and close. A moment later Harry Zeeb hurried into the alley and turned uptown toward the back door of Childers' mercantile. He looked around just before he reached it and saw Lane standing there. He broke into a run, turned in toward the loading dock at the rear of the mercantile store and disappeared from Lane's view.

It was dangerous to push the town this way. It vastly increased the danger that someone would shoot him down, from ambush or from behind.

But he was enjoying it. There was bitter satisfaction in seeing the panic that overwhelmed each man he pushed.

Lane knew he couldn't kill a town. He couldn't kill every man who had helped kill Jess. But he could make them sweat.

CHAPTER 8

Saralee Vargas still turned cold with horror when she remembered the night of the lynching six months before. She had neither seen the hanging nor the body afterward. But she had seen the way righteous outrage over the manner of Lorina Newkirk's death grew within the men of the town until it became an ugly, almost obscene thing that had nothing to do with righteousness. And she had seen Jess Sauer dragged out of the jail, screaming his innocence, screaming for justice and a proper trial.

She blamed the townsmen bitterly for what they had done, but she was also horrified and personally ashamed. Because she knew that she, as well as most of the other women in town, had contributed. The women's outrage had fed the flames growing in the men. It had given tacit approval to their anger by permitting it. The women could have calmed their men, could have prevented lawlessness by doing so. But they had an anger of their own, an anger that one of them could have been brutally assaulted and killed right here in town. Each told herself it could have happened to her.

Saralee knew now that it could not. It could only have happened to one woman in the town. It could only have happened to Lorina.

Lorina hadn't been able to meet a man without wanting him to show interest in her. It fed some need, some obscure hunger for importance, some thirst for reassurance. She flirted subtly. She flaunted herself with equal subtlety. She made men want her by letting them think the idea was not as preposterous as it might seem.

She had made the stranger notice her right here in the hotel dining room. Saralee had seen the way he watched Lorina when she got up to leave. She had seen the way Lorina's oblique glance brushed softly over him as she went out through the door.

Now she gathered up the dishes left by Lane Sauer, slipping her hand deftly beneath them so that the letter was between the plate and her hand.

She carried the dishes to the kitchen. When she put them down, her back was to the cook, her body concealing the letter as she slipped it into the neckline of her dress.

The gesture committed her. She would help Lane Sauer, at least this much. She would get the letter to Meyer and ask him to mail it at the next town he reached.

She went back into the dining room, which was deserted now. She crossed it to the lobby door. Maynard Brooks had his back to her. Otherwise the lobby was deserted.

Hurriedly, almost silently, she climbed the stairs, avoiding the one that creaked. She reached the top and hurried along the hall.

She knocked softly at Meyer's door. His high, thin voice said peevishly, "Come in."

She opened it. She saw a flicker of interest come into his eyes at her unexpected appearance here. She withdrew the letter, feeling a flush crawl up into her face, confused and flustered because it did. She said, "I wonder if you would do something for me." She closed the door behind her.

68

He grinned. "Anything, little lady. Just anything you say."

Her discomfiture increased. He was sitting on the unmade bed. He had removed his coat and collar. She could see the sweat that had darkened his shirt beneath his armpits. His face looked slightly oily, and he needed a shave.

She said, "I want to mail a letter, but I don't want to mail it here. I . . . you understand, don't you? My father doesn't approve of what I'm doing . . . I mean . . ."

He leered. "Sure I understand. You just bet I do."

She crossed the room timidly and handed the letter to him. She had hoped he might just put it into his pocket without looking at it but he did not. He studied the address and the handwriting and when he looked up again his expression had completely changed. He looked frightened now. Uneasy. He asked, "What's goin' on in this town anyway? This ain't your letter. It's in a man's writing and it's addressed to someone named Sauer. That's the name of the stranger that got beat up last night. What are you trying to put over on me anyway?"

She said, "Please. It's important. It's a letter to his family."

"Then why don't he mail it downstairs like anybody else? Why pick on me? I got a job to keep. I got to stay on the good side of these people here. Something's going on that I don't like. To hell with it, lady. Mail your letter yourself."

He was sweating heavily now. His eyes had a trapped, scared look. Saralee said softly, "No one's going to know. All you have to do—"

"Why should I? I don't owe you nothin'. Why should I stick my neck out for you?"

His voice had risen steadily until she was sure it could

69

be heard outside the room. She stared at him. She forced herself to smile but the smile felt like a grimace on her face. Words came to her lips that startled her, that made her ashamed. "Because . . . well, if you do this for me, I might . . ." She couldn't go on. Not even to save Sauer's life. She hated the little man suddenly, hated the way he licked his lips, hated the hot look that came into his eyes.

For a moment she thought he was going to get up off the bed and grab her. She started to retreat, then firmly forced herself to hold her ground. A man's life hung in the balance here. A good man's life.

Fear fought a battle with desire in his eyes. At last he nodded sullenly. He said, "All right. But next time I come in town . . ."

She nodded, unable now to meet his eyes. Trembling almost uncontrollably, she crossed to the door, opened it and stepped into the hall. She glanced worriedly at the head of the stairs. She saw no one, but just then she heard the squeak of the tread she had avoided earlier. Someone was on the stairs. Someone had seen her go into Meyer's room.

For a long moment she stood frozen there. She understood the mood of the men in town. She knew their guilt and their fear of discovery. She knew to what lengths some of them would go to keep Saguaro's secret from the outside world. Her knees began to tremble and her chest felt cold and tight.

Silently, walking on her toes, she crept toward the head of the stairs. When she was close enough to see all the way down, she saw that they were empty. No one was in sight.

Their emptiness caused a chill to run along her spine.

Slowly, a step at a time, she descended, avoiding automatically the tread that squeaked.

Maynard Brooks was not at the desk. No one was in the lobby. It looked peaceful and harmless in the morning sun that streamed through the windows and glared on the white tile floor.

Swiftly, almost running, she returned to the dining room. Reaching it, she sank weakly into a chair. Her body was damp with perspiration, but in spite of that she felt cold as ice.

Frowning, she tried to conquer her fear. Lane Sauer was alone here. No one would help him. No one but her.

Yet even she would be no help to him if she did not conquer her fear. She forced a steadiness to come to her hands. She forced her numb mind to function.

Why was she willing to help him, she asked herself. Why? She didn't even know the man.

Turning her head, she saw Lane Sauer sitting in one of the veranda chairs. He looked relaxed, almost indolent in spite of his battered face. She remembered suddenly his strong, muscled body which she had bandaged for him last night. And she felt her face grow hot.

He was worth helping, but there was more to it than that. If she helped him, she realized, she would also help herself. She would, perhaps, cleanse some of her own guilt caused by the outrage she had shared with the men of Saguaro that awful night. She would, through Lane, find new courage—perhaps enough to leave Saguaro for good.

She would help her father too. For an instant her face softened with pity for Severo. Losing her mother had been hard for him. She had not blamed him for drinking to forget. That was sometimes the way of a man. She only hoped that when she died a man would grieve for her that deeply.

No, she hadn't blamed him at first, when the drinking had been a way of grieving for the dead. But later, it had become more than that. It had turned into a kind of flight, into a kind of hiding from reality and from the world. He drank because he couldn't face himself or face the world.

She'd brought him out of that, a year and a half ago, by telling him if he did not stop drinking she would leave. And then, six months ago, he'd let himself be dragged into the town's angry hysteria. He'd let himself become a part of that lusting mob. He'd gone along, dragging Sauer down River Street in the dead of night toward the rope that waited on the cottonwood.

Severo Vargas had not been the only man in Saguaro who had thereafter numbed himself with liquor to forget. But with Severo drinking was not an occasional thing. It was continuous. The only time she saw him sober was in the morning when he stumbled out of bed, disheveled, dirty and sick, and headed for the saloon to wait for its opening.

He was no longer a man, she thought, only a sodden animal. But if she could now force him to join her in helping Lane . . . There might be hope for him. The danger—the very act of trying to atone for the wrong six months before—these things might redeem him as nothing else could do.

She studied Sauer's face, her own growing softer as she did. It was a strong face, a rugged, roughhewn face, handsome in spite of the marks the beating had put on it. The eyes were deep-set, intelligent and kind. But they could lose that kindness too. They could be as hard as steel.

His mouth was, this morning, puffed unrecognizably. But she remembered the way it had been before. Firm, but looking as though it might curve into a smile at any time.

She shook her head impatiently. She was mooning like an idiot. If she was going to help him, she would not do it sitting here. She left the dining room and crossed the lobby toward the door. From a corner of her eye, she caught a glimpse of Maynard Brooks at the desk, watching her.

Sam Meyer stared at the closed door for a long time after Saralee went out. The letter seemed to burn his sweating hand. Yet for the moment he ignored it, letting his mind indulge in fantasies about the next trip he would take to Saguaro a month from now.

God, he thought, that was a beautiful girl! He'd admired her ever since she'd started working in the hotel dining room more than a year ago. These Mexican girls . . . they had warmth, a softness rarely found in other women you saw out here on the frontier. Saloon girls were hard and brittle or tiredly cynical. The good women were prim and bony with a tight-lipped righteousness that made a man go cold.

He felt the letter in his hand and looked at it. He couldn't understand why it frightened him so. It was only a letter. No one need know she had given it to him. He could take it with him and mail it and a month from now come back and claim what that girl had promised him. . . .

He licked his lips. He looked at the letter again. What if she had been seen coming into his room? He got up and the bed creaked thunderously. He crossed to the door and silently opened it. He peered into the hall, then quickly closed the door again.

No one had been in the hall. But what if someone had been there before? What if someone had been listening at the door?

He went back to the bed and sat down on the edge of it. He slid the letter under the mattress almost quietly. To hell with it. He didn't know what it was about the town this trip that made him so edgy and uneasy. He couldn't understand his fear. But it was there, cold as a chunk of ice lying where his heart should be.

He got up, walked to the window and stared down into the street. It was already hot down there and the heat had begun to creep into the room. The street looked peaceful, even drowsy. Yet a menace seemed to emanate from it, a menace that was real even if it was something he could not understand.

He turned his head and stared at the bed, at the place he had put the letter. He thought of Saralee again. Once he'd mailed the letter she would probably refuse what she'd practically promised him. Practically was right, he thought ruefully. He'd been so anxious to believe . . . Hell, she hadn't really promised anything. She'd only hinted at it. And the way her eyes had looked as she did . . . She'd been half scared to death.

Scared of what, he wondered. Of him? Why should she be scared of him? He was just a fat little man traveling around selling whisky to the saloons. She was a couple of inches taller than he and probably stronger too.

His hands began to shake again. Something was in that letter that could get him killed. Like the stranger had damn near got killed last night.

He crossed the room to the washbasin and poured some water in it. He washed, and shaved, then, without changing his shirt, affixed the celluloid collar to it and put on his greasy tie.

He wished it was noon. He wished the damn stage was in so that he could leave.

He began to pace nervously back and forth, occasionally glancing at the bed where the letter was. The exertion made him sweat even more heavily and it didn't help his nerves.

An idea came to him. Why couldn't he open the letter? If he soaked the flap, he could open it without tearing it. If anybody ever questioned him, he could say the letter got soaked with sweat just carrying it.

He hesitated a moment, then resolutely crossed the room to the bed. He withdrew the letter with a shaking hand. He went to the washbasin and dipped a finger into the water, afterward moistening the flap with it. He waited impatiently for the water to loosen the glue. Several times he glanced toward the door as though half expecting to be surprised.

At last he slid a finger underneath the flap. It pulled loose reluctantly. He opened the letter and looked at it. It read:

Dear Pa:

I got to Saguaro and I got bad news for you. Jess is dead. He was accused of killing some woman here and because he had some brush scratches on his face they strung him up. Turned out next day that he hadn't done nothing, but that didn't help Jess then. I think you and the boys had ought to come here right away. This is a real mean town and I think they're fixing to kill me too. If they do, you see they pay for it. I'm sorry to be the one to send you this bad news. I'm sorry for Jess and I'm going to try and put a marker on his grave. There ain't no God in this town and no preacher either, but I'll say some words over Jess the way I know you'd want me to.

Your son,
Lane

Meyer's hands shook almost uncontrollably as he put the letter back into the envelope. He licked the flap, closed it and returned it to the place under the mattress. He looked down at his knees and realized they were shaking too. If anybody ever found out he had read the letter . . . If anyone caught him trying to get it out . . .

Damn that girl! Damn her to hell, promising him, letting him think she would . . . Hell, she was trying to get him killed!

He began to pace back and forth again. He felt as though this room was a cage, but he was afraid to go out of it. As scared as he was, if someone said "letter" to him he'd jump a mile and give the whole thing away.

He heard heavy steps coming up the stairs. He heard the tread squeak even through his closed door. He heard the steps approach his room.

Too late to lock it now. He held his breath, waiting, waiting for the knock to sound on it.

CHAPTER 9

Maynard Brooks watched closely from the lobby door as Saralee Vargas served Sauer. He did not miss her nervousness and fear. He thought Sauer must have said something to her, for she started and almost spilled his soup as she put it down in front of him.

He ducked out of sight once when Sauer turned his head. When Sauer finished eating, and took out his pipe and tobacco pouch, Brooks started to turn away but stopped when his eye caught a glimpse of the letter underneath Sauer's tobacco pouch. He saw it go under the plate.

He went back to the desk, frowning. He watched Sauer come out of the dining room and go through the lobby door onto the hotel veranda. He left the desk and returned to the dining-room door, standing so that he could see only the table at which Sauer had sat. He saw Saralee come and gather up the dishes and knew she had the letter beneath the plate.

He returned to the desk again. When he heard her coming out of the dining room, he deliberately turned his back to her. She went up the stairs. He could hear her even though she avoided the tread that squeaked.

Brooks was forty-eight. He owned this hotel. Every cent he had in the world was tied up in it. A lifetime of working and saving and doing without was represented by it. It was a good beginning. Someday, Saguaro was going to be the capital of a new state to be formed out of this territory. A railroad would come through here. The town would grow. He could be a wealthy man.

But not if the story of the lynching got out. Something like that would ruin Saguaro's chances of becoming the state capital. Saguaro would become deserted in a year or two. The hotel would sit here and deteriorate and Brooks would be broke again.

Angrily he considered the prospect. It wasn't going to happen. He wasn't going to let it happen. Not if he had to kill Lane Sauer himself.

He'd denied himself everything that made life worth-while to acquire this hotel. He'd never married because he knew a wife would slow him down. Now he faced the prospect of losing everything and it made his stomach knot with fear.

He caught himself thinking of Lorina Newkirk in spite of the resolve he'd made six months ago never to think of her again. He'd needed her the way a man dying of thirst on the desert needs a drink. She represented all the things he had denied himself along the way. And he realized something he had never realized before. He had loved her more deeply than he had ever loved anything or anyone. He would even have given up the hotel if she had asked him to. He would have gone away with her.

He would not believe, even now, that her relationship with the other men of the town had been the same as it had with him. They were only casual friends, who visited her occasionally to talk and to look at her. When she had been killed . . . when he'd seen her body lying in the undertaking parlor at the back of the furniture store . . . He remembered still the numb shock that had frozen him. He remembered the rage that had grown so monstrously out of the shock.

He would have killed Jess Sauer with his own two hands if he could. He'd tried to reach the man when they dragged him out of the jail. He'd failed because of the men crowding around Sauer, blocking him.

He was glad, the next day, that he hadn't reached the man. He hadn't laid a hand on him all the way to the cottonwood. He hadn't touched the rope, or the horse, or the whip that sent the horse plunging away. He could tell himself, with perfect truth, that he had been a spectator, not a participant. He had been there, that was all. No guilt attached to him.

He therefore did not deserve to be ruined by what had happened that night. He deserved it less than anyone in town.

Lane Sauer was trying to get a letter out. He had tried mailing one at the post office. Now he was trying to get one out through Saralee and Sam Meyer. Saralee was up there right now giving it to Sam.

He left the desk and quietly climbed the stairs. At the head of them he stopped. Meyer's door was closed but he heard the whisky drummer's high, thin voice, "Why should I? I don't owe you nothin'. Why should I stick my neck out for you?"

He heard the murmur of the girl's voice but not her words. He began his soft retreat back down the stairs.

He heard Meyer's door open. Swiftly he descended the remaining stairs, completely forgetting the one that squeaked. Sweating, he ran across the lobby and ducked into his office behind the desk.

Peering cautiously out the door, he saw Saralee come down the stairs and hurry into the dining room.

He returned to the desk. The thought of the letter, now upstairs in Meyer's hands, was almost intolerable, but he didn't want to take the chance of having Saralee see him go up after it. Wait until she leaves, he told himself. There's plenty of time before the stage gets in.

The wait seemed endless but at last Saralee came out of the dining room, crossed the lobby and went outside. Brooks left the desk immediately. He climbed the stairs and knocked on Meyer's door.

There was no sound inside the room. He knocked again. Then he put his hand on the knob and opened the door.

Meyer stood halfway across the room, staring at him with eyes that were wide with fear. Brooks nodded affably. "Good morning, Mr. Meyer. I just saw the waitress coming out of here. Was she bothering you?"

The man shook his head violently. Brooks said, "Do you mind if I ask what she wanted here?"

Meyer's face was white. His hands were shaking. He seemed able to find no words.

Brooks dropped all pretense. He said softly, "Give me the letter, Mr. Meyer, and I'll give it to the sheriff."

"The sheriff?"

"Of course. Sauer is an outlaw. Didn't you know that? He's writing his brothers to come. When they get here, he's planning to loot the town."

He could see two conflicting emotions in Meyer's face. Relief, because the story gave him a way out, and increased fear because he knew the truth.

Brooks said, his voice still soft but suddenly very cold, "We like you here in Saguaro, Mr. Meyer. You get a lot of business. It would be too bad if you were to say things about Saguaro that weren't true."

Meyer stammered, "I wouldn't . . . I don't. . . . What could I say about anything? I try to mind my own business,

Mr. Brooks. A salesman has to mind his own business. All I do is sell whisky. I don't talk about anything."

Brooks nodded approvingly. "Then give me the letter, Mr. Meyer. And forget you ever saw it. Forget you read it. Then you can keep coming back to Saguaro. Your business might improve. If the saloonkeepers knew you were friendly toward us here . . ."

Meyer hesitated between denying he had the letter and admitting it. At last he turned, reached under the mattress and withdrew the letter. He handed it to Brooks, who said, "You won't regret this, Mr. Meyer. Just put the whole thing out of your mind and everything will be all right."

Meyer nodded violently. He seemed weak with relief. He sank down on the bed.

Brooks put the letter in his pocket and went out, closing the door softly behind him. He stood for a moment in the hall, then went briskly down the stairs.

He didn't have to study the envelope flap to know Meyer had opened it. But he also knew Meyer would keep still. He went out and crossed the street to Holt Childers' mercantile. Lane Sauer was still sitting on the hotel veranda, looking relaxed and indolent. He could feel Sauer's eyes on his back all the way across the street.

He felt his anger stir. Damn the man, where did he get the gall to sit there baiting the town, daring them to try and get rid of him? An unexplainable uneasiness touched him as he climbed the two steps to the door of Holt Childers' store. Maybe it wasn't gall. Maybe Sauer knew something the rest of the town did not. Maybe he had help coming. The letters might have been written for the purpose of throwing the townspeople off their guard.

He knew that was ridiculous immediately. Sauer had just found out about the lynching this morning. He couldn't have summoned help.

81

Childers was at the rear of the store talking to Riker. Childers' face was red with anger. Both men stopped talking when Brooks came in.

Brooks walked along the aisle to the rear of the store. He took the letter from his pocket and handed it to Childers. "He got Saralee to give this to Meyer. I got it from Meyer, but he read it, judging from the way he acts."

Childers frowned and tore open the envelope. He took out the letter and read it aloud. After that, he studied the flap, nodding as he did. "He read it all right. Wet the flap and opened it." He peered closely at Brooks. "Think Meyer will keep his mouth shut?"

Brooks nodded. "I think so. I reminded him that he got a lot of business out of this town. Besides, Meyer hasn't got the guts to say anything. He saw the way Sauer was beat up."

Riker rumbled, "Maybe I'd better go over and have a little talk with him."

Childers frowned at him. "You think your goddam fists are the answer to everything. Don't worry about Meyer. He'll keep still."

Brooks said, "What about Sauer? That's what I want to know. If we let him get on that stage . . ."

"How do you know he's going to get on the stage?"

"What would you do if you were in his shoes? Hell, he knows he's not safe here. And besides, he knows what he came to find out. He's smart enough to realize he can't take on the town by himself. So he'll take the stage. He'll try and get out to go for help."

"I wonder how many brothers he's got?"

Brooks shrugged. It didn't matter how many brothers Sauer had. What did matter was that he must not be allowed to leave. Brooks said, "Even if he brings his brothers here, what can he do? That's not what I'm scared of. What worries me is what will happen to this town if the news gets out. We'd just as well forget about being the state capital and start worrying about staying alive in a town with no people in it."

Childers nodded. Riker stood looking from one to the other, glowering uncertainly as though he did not quite understand the implications of their words. At last he growled, "Let me take care of the son of a bitch."

Childers looked at him pityingly. "What would you do, beat him to death with your fists?"

Riker's scowl deepened. Brooks thought he was a pig, a stupid, greedy pig. But even a pig can be dangerous. Riker was like a wild boar, mean, unpredictable, not too smart and appallingly powerful. Riker grumbled, "What the hell would be wrong with that? I can bait him into a fight, and then break the son of a bitch in two."

Childers hesitated. Brooks said, "I don't know how you'd manage it. He's got his gun. Manus came in this morning and got it from me. He gave it back to him."

For a moment Riker seemed uncertain. Brooks said, "One thing's sure, you can't beat him to the draw. That gun's been used."

Childers said musingly, "Wait a minute. Maybe we can work this out."

Riker said, "We could get someone to shoot him if he goes for his gun. Even Manus couldn't quarrel with that. I won't have a gun. If Sauer goes for his, anybody'd be right in shooting him."

Childers said, "Who would you get?"

"Murphy. His store's right across the street from the hotel. He could leave his door open and shoot through it with a rifle. He could even use a rest to be sure he didn't miss."

Childers left the pair and began to pace uneasily back

and forth. Brooks watched him, thinking that even though the plan was crude, it was workable. If Sauer touched his gun he would be drawing against an unarmed man. And if Murphy killed him while he was doing it, if he waited until Sauer's gun was in his hand . . .

They'd be rid of Sauer. The danger of exposure would be gone. He could feel relief already touching him. Saguaro wouldn't be ruined if Sauer died.

Childers stopped pacing. He asked, "What about Sauer's family?"

Brooks shrugged. "We don't notify them because we don't know where they are. Sooner or later some of them will show up. When they do, Manus will tell 'em what happened. They'll probably never nose out what happened six months ago."

"What if they do?"

Brooks looked at him. He said pityingly, "What if they do? Good God, man, we can't guarantee everything. If they find out what happened then we'll face that problem when it comes up. This is the problem we've got to face today."

Childers nodded reluctantly. "I guess you're right. But it seems awfully crude, just shooting him down like that."

Riker stood waiting silently, an expression of expectation on his face. Brooks knew he was thinking about getting his hands on Sauer again. Sauer had marked him up some last night, and the fact that he had gave Brooks an obscure feeling of pleasure. From what he had heard about the fight, Sauer might have beaten Riker if Murphy hadn't butted in.

He glanced from Riker to Childers. Childers had the kind of mind that rejected any plan unless it was complex. If Childers had his way, he'd try to plan some kind of complicated accident.

Childers asked worriedly, "What if it doesn't work? What if Sauer comes out of it alive?"

"How the hell can he? Murphy's one of the best shots in town. If he has a rest for his rifle, I don't see how he can miss."

"A lot of things could happen. What if Sauer steps behind the coach?"

Brooks didn't like Childers very well. He thought the town should have made him mayor instead of the storekeeper. He thought of himself as being the most important man in town. He said with exaggerated patience, "Then suppose you come up with a better plan."

Childers frowned. At last he nodded reluctantly. "All right. I guess it's worth a try." He glanced at Riker. "Just be damn sure, Otto, that he doesn't get behind the coach."

Riker grinned. "He won't." He stood waiting for a moment, as though expecting some further instructions. Brooks said, "Talk to Murphy. Get it all arranged."

Riker nodded. He turned away and shuffled toward the front of the store. From the rear he looked like an ungainly bear.

The silence between Brooks and Childers was awkward now. Brooks nodded shortly at the storekeeper and headed toward the front of the store.

He was angry at himself because, like most of the others in town, he brought everything to the mayor. He had brought the letter here, for Childers to act upon.

And he was also a little shocked at himself. He and Childers and Riker had planned Sauer's death the way they might have planned a poker game.

He shook his head a little as he went out into the blazing heat. He glanced at Sauer, still sitting on the hotel veranda across the street. He hated the man suddenly, hated him because by his very presence here he had made the planned murder necessary.

He crossed the street and climbed the veranda steps without looking at Sauer. He told himself firmly, that it wasn't murder at all. It was self-defense. Sauer would ruin them all if he could. It was their right to protect themselves.

But he wasn't convinced. And he was glad someone else was going to do the dirty work.

CHAPTER 10

Sitting on the veranda, Lane Sauer saw Saralee Vargas come out of the hotel. She crossed the street and headed toward home without looking at him. After that, he saw Riker come from the livery barn downstreet and walk to Childers' mercantile. Riker favored him with one murderous glance. Lane stared back at him steadily. Scowling, Riker went into the store across the street.

Lane had never known a man like Riker before. Riker was just plain mean. If Childers hadn't stopped him last night he'd have gone on beating Lane until he was dead. Riker, he thought, would be a good man to watch today because he would probably be the one they got to do their dirty work. He'd be too stupid to realize he was being used.

The door behind Lane opened and Maynard Brooks came out. He hurried across the street without looking aside at Lane.

Lane frowned faintly as he watched Brooks go into Childers' store. Brooks's hurrying to the mayor so soon after Saralee's departure made him wonder what Brooks had seen. He might have seen Saralee pick up the letter from beneath the plate. Or he might have seen her going up the stairs to Meyer's room.

Still frowning, he glanced up and down the street. It drowsed in the hot morning sun and yet, like yesterday, he felt menace emanating from it, menace that was tangible and real, that he knew was not imaginary. This town would kill him today if it could. He didn't know how it would happen, or when, but he knew it would. They were planning it across the street.

He looked relaxed, but he was not. Every nerve, every muscle was tight. Pain from his broken ribs was throbbing and continuous and it hurt to breathe. His mouth was puffy and dry and one of his eyes was nearly closed. Riker had softened him up for the town. He wouldn't be as fast or as strong as he should be today.

Riker came out of the store. He paused on the walk a moment and looked across at Sauer again. He was no longer scowling but at this distance Lane couldn't make out what his expression was.

He turned and shambled down the street toward the livery barn. At the gunsmith's shop, he stopped, opened the door and went in.

The trouble would come from Riker, Lane thought. And maybe from the gunsmith too. He frowned puzzledly, thinking that this was too direct, too simple to readily believe. They must have a better plan than simply turning Riker loose on him again.

He got painfully to his feet, worrying about the letter and knowing he had to find out if Brooks had intercepted it. He crossed the lobby and climbed the stairs quickly, wanting this to be done before Brooks returned.

He knocked lightly on Meyer's door. He waited a moment, then knocked again. The door opened and Meyer stood framed in it.

The man's face was a ghastly shade of gray. It was dripping with sweat. He was shaking violently. Lane

88

pushed him aside, went in and closed the door. He said, "You look scared."

Meyer moistened his lips with his tongue. He nodded violently. "I am scared. I don't want nothin' to do with you. I ain't done anything. I'm just a salesman and I wasn't even here . . ." He stopped and wet his lips again as he realized he had said too much.

Lane said, "She gave you the letter then. And you read it. What else?"

"What else? What else is there? I don't want no part of it. I—"

"Where's the letter now?"

"Brooks took it. He came in here like somebody'd told him I had it and took it away from me. You get out of here, mister. I got to make a living and if this town's cut out of my territory I'll lose my job."

Lane stared at the frightened man. Fright was catching, he thought. Right now he was pretty scared himself. He hadn't succeeded in getting a letter out and he knew dismally that he wasn't going to succeed. Furthermore, he knew they weren't going to let him get on that stage. There might be decent men in Saguaro, although he doubted it in view of what had happened to Jess. Yet even if there were, they wouldn't do anything to stop the others from killing him. They hadn't stopped the mob from lynching Jess.

Gloomily he faced the probability that he'd die here in Saguaro with Jess unavenged. Ultimately, one or more of his brothers would come to find out what had happened to him, but they might not succeed in doing so. The town would have learned something from his own arrival here. Next time the truth would be difficult if not impossible to pry out of anyone. Next time they'd be on guard.

He stared speculatively at Meyer, feeling something like ice in the middle of his chest. Meyer knew the truth. He knew where the Sauer ranch was from reading the address on the letter. If he would. . . .

He shook his head slightly. Meyer wouldn't dare talk to anyone. If he did, the townspeople would know it had been him.

Meyer said thinly, "For God's sake, get out of here! If they knew you were here . . . they'd kill me. Just like they're going to . . ." He stopped.

Lane nodded. He turned, opened the door and looked out into the hall. It was empty, so he stepped through and closed the door softly behind him. He walked along the hall to his own room, opened the door and went in.

He couldn't blame Meyer, he guessed. The man hadn't been a part of the lynching and there was no reason why he should have to suffer because of it.

Absently he touched his gun. It might not save his life, he thought, but there were five bullets in it. Five bullets to avenge Jess's death. He owed it to Jess and to himself that each one found a mark.

He paced to the window and stared down into the street. Brooks was halfway across, heading this way. He did not look up.

At least, thought Lane, the whisky drummer was safe. Brooks hadn't seen him go to Meyer's room. Meyer was safe unless he gave himself away.

He began to pace nervously back and forth, unmindful of the ever-increasing heat. His mind was like an animal in a cage, probing, seeking, trying to find some way out, examining each possibility before going on to the next. He spent half an hour pacing back and forth, but he found no way out because, he told himself, there wasn't one. The whole town was against him. Saralee Vargas had tried to help but she had done all she could. A woman couldn't help him against men with guns.

He thought of the sheriff but without hope. Manus hadn't been willing to kill any of the townsmen in defense of his prisoner. It wasn't likely he was going to change now. Besides, he had a stake in this too. If the truth came out, he'd be without a job. He'd be branded for the rest of his life as the sheriff who had given a prisoner to a mob.

To Lane, it seemed impossible that he had been here in Saguaro less than a whole day and night. He felt as though he had been here for weeks. And there were still a couple of hours left before the stage got in. The thought came to him that he ought to be doing something special with those two hours because they were going to be his last.

Saralee did not speak to Lane Sauer as she passed him on the veranda of the hotel. To do so would, she realized, call attention to them both.

Head down, she hurried along the street toward home. She would have to return to the hotel half an hour before noon. Until then, her time was her own. She could feel Lane Sauer's glance upon her back. She wanted to turn her head and look at him, but she did not.

The Spanish section of Saguaro was as quiet as the rest of it. Everyone seemed to be waiting until Lane Sauer would be gone. They were staying indoors because none of them wanted to look him in the face.

Saralee went up the short walk to her own adobe house. There was a gallery in front, running the width of the house, its roof supported by stout spruce posts. Saralee tried the door and found it barred. She knocked lightly, more heavily when her first knocks drew no response. At last she heard a groan inside.

She called, "Father! Open the door. Father!"

She heard another groan. After what seemed an interminable time, she heard the bar raised and the door swung open, creaking slightly as it did.

She went inside. All the shutters were closed and it was dark, almost as dark as night. She closed the door behind her and barred it again. She looked at her father, now sitting at the table with his head down and buried in his folded arms. She asked, "What's the matter? Why are you hiding here in a darkened house?"

"I told him. I told him about the lynching six months ago. I was sick and he caught me leaving here. . . ." He raised his head and stared at her, eyes wide with terror. "They'll kill me when they find out it was me that talked."

"How do you know they'll find out?"

"They'll find out all right. They find out everything."

They probably would, too, Saralee thought. Saguaro was a changed town since the lynching six months ago. Nobody trusted anybody else. There was always a lot of whispering going around.

But kill Severo? Why would they want to kill someone as harmless as he? To keep him from babbling again, she realized. The men in this town would do anything to keep their secret from the world.

She sat down at the table across from him. "How drunk are you? Can you think? Can you talk?"

"I don't know! I don't know!" He raised his head. "What are we going to do?"

"Get out of town," she said practically.

Severo laughed bitterly. "You make it sound so simple, so easy. How do you expect we can manage it?"

"By getting on the stage today. They won't dare hurt us in broad daylight in the middle of River Street. Besides, they're going to be too busy with the stranger to pay any attention to us."

Severo didn't answer her. He let his head drop to the table again. Saralee sat down beside him and shook his shoulder with her hand. "Father, listen to me! Perhaps I am foolish, as you think. Perhaps it is impossible. But do you think drinking yourself into unconsciousness every day is less impossible?"

"They'll kill us."

"Maybe. Maybe they will kill us, along with him. But it's our only hope. If we don't go, you'll go on drinking. Nothing will ever make you stop. And I'll spend my life picking you out of the gutter and bringing you home."

She stopped and stared at him, trying to make her face cold. She went on, "I want more than that. Mother would have wanted more than that for me, and more for you. I want a husband, Father, and I want children. I want those things badly enough to leave you if you haven't the courage to go with me."

He raised his head. He looked at her with eyes that could not hold hers. He licked his lips. He tried to say yes. She could see him trying but he couldn't get it out.

Saralee felt tears forming behind her eyes. Partly they were tears of pity for Severo, for what he had become. Partly they were tears of anger because she knew if Severo didn't go, neither could she.

She said urgently, "Listen to me, Father! This stranger, this Lane Sauer . . . he is a strong man and he has his gun back now. Perhaps those who would kill him will not succeed. Perhaps he will fight them off and get on the stage. If we are there and ready and if he does fight them off, then we can get on the stagecoach too."

He gave no sign that he had heard. Saralee realized she had deceived him and wondered if he knew she had. She did not intend to be there at the stage depot only in case Sauer fought them off. She wanted to be there to help him, with her presence to help him, and to board the stage no matter what the townspeople did or tried to do.

She sighed helplessly because Severo did not raise his head. He was too terrified to think, she realized. Liquor had dissolved a little of him each day until now there was nothing left. No courage. No shame. No will. No sense of decency. She felt tears burning against the back of her eyes because this was so.

Anger began to rise in her. Anger at the men of the town who had goaded Severo into participating in the lynching, anger at those who had goaded him into drinking afterward. But there was anger for her father, too, and for herself.

She could give up, soft with sympathy for Severo, for the problem that made him drink. She could go on, earning the money for their food, for their rent, for his liquor that he could not do without. She could die a fat, ugly old maid without ever having borne a child or known the fulfillment God meant women to experience.

Or else, she thought, she could *make* him do this thing. He did not want salvation. He did not want to be saved. She must force him to be saved!

She stared at his touseled, matted, uncut hair, at his dirty hands, at his soiled and wrinkled clothes. He just didn't care any more.

He was like a pig on sour mash, who ate of it and staggered away to fall drunkenly into the mud, who slept and got up to eat of the sour mash again.

94

He would be this way, furthermore, as long as the lynching of Jess Sauer remained a secret from the world. Only if it came out, only if it was widely known, could he find peace.

CHAPTER 11

Pacing back and forth in his room, Lane felt stubborn determination growing in him, fed by anger and by the helplessness that had troubled him ever since his arrival here. Until now he had wanted only one thing, to find out what happened to Jess. Now he wanted more.

He had succeeded as far as he had gone. He had found out how Jess had died. He had learned that practically every man in Saguaro had participated. But if they killed him today, it would be as though he had never been here at all. The secret of Jess's death would remain secret. The guilty, bloody hands in the town would not be cleansed but only bloodied all over again.

His pacing became faster, his scowl deeper and angrier. How? How could he snatch success from failure? How could he succeed even though he died? He had tried twice to get a letter out and had failed both times.

He knew one thing for sure. He could not do this alone. Somewhere in Saguaro he had to find a man with the courage to help him get out of town alive, or, failing that, to make his death meaningful at least.

He stopped pacing suddenly. If, by some miracle, he did get out . . . what exactly would he do? Come back with his father and brothers? Exact vengeance from each man who had taken part? He shook his head slowly. No. It seemed to him that only the law could effectively avenge lawlessness.

But the law would not function against a whole community. Therefore it must be done through publicity, through public opinion all over the territory. The story and the names of the men involved must be printed in newspapers everywhere, to be carried like a brand by each man until he died, an indelible brand that even years of exemplary living could not erase.

One more thing—Jess's body must go home. Jess must not lie here in this guilty, bloody town beside the killer for whose crime he died. His body must come home, to lie on the grassy hill behind the house with those of his mother and the baby sister who had died when she was born.

He stopped by the window and stared at the building across the street. Painted on one of the second-story windows were the words "Thomas Kemmerer, Atty. at Law."

His eyes narrowed. He tried to see through the dirty windows into the office beyond. He could see a desk and the dim shape of a man behind it and that was all.

He turned suddenly and left the room. If he was going to find a man in Saguaro without guilt on his soul, it would most likely be a man of the law. Perhaps Kemmerer would be the one.

He hurried down the stairs and across the lobby. Time was getting short. He tried to appear unconcerned as he crossed the street but he was far from unconcerned. At any moment, he knew, a bullet might come out of nowhere to seek his heart. A spot in the middle of his back ached as though in expectation of such a bullet striking it.

There was an outside stairway at the side of the build-

97

ing leading to the offices on the second floor. Lane climbed it, aware of what a fine target he made doing so. He ducked into the door at the top hurriedly. The unknown, he thought ruefully, was harder on a man than the known. The unknown could break his nerve.

He smiled grimly to himself as he stared along the hall. The town might kill him, but he was damned if they were going to break his nerve. And if they did not kill him, he'd be waiting for the stage when it came in.

He walked along the hall until he came to a door bearing Thomas Kemmerer's name. Underneath the name he saw the words "County Judge." He knocked.

A deep voice called, "Come in," and he opened the door and went inside. He closed the door behind him and stood with his back to it, staring at the man behind the desk.

The man was elderly, sixty or older he guessed. He had white hair. He was of medium size and his face and hands were brown from the desert sun—as though he hadn't always worked inside—as though he'd once held a circuit judge's job.

Lane said, "I'm Lane Sauer."

The man looked up. He nodded. "I know." His eyes were blue, almost the blue of a robin's egg, thought Lane. Maybe this was the man he had been looking for, the honest man who would help.

"What else do you know?"

The judge's eyes sharpened slightly. They studied Lane a moment carefully. At last Kemmerer said, "I know that you're Jess Sauer's brother and that you've come to find out what happened to him. You've found out. Now you want to know how to get out of town alive."

Lane nodded. His eyes held respect for the judge's concise, knife-sharp appraisal of him. He asked, "How *can* I get out?"

Kemmerer shook his head regretfully. "I'm afraid you can't. This is a shamed and guilty town, Mr. Sauer. Some of us might let you go, but the majority would never stand for it."

"You say, 'some of us.' Do you mean to say *you* helped hang Jess? You, a judge?" His voice had suddenly turned cold.

Kemmerer's face flushed slowly. His eyes avoided Lane's. He nodded silently and when he spoke his voice was scarcely audible. "To my everlasting shame, I did. I helped. I presided over the mock trial that was held."

He raised his eyes and forced them to meet Lane's. He said, deliberately holding his gaze steady and unwavering, "I don't want you to get the wrong idea. When I say 'mock trial,' I mean just that. There was no semblance of legality to it. Your brother had no chance to hear a verdict other than the guilty one. He was a dead man before I called the trial to order."

"Why . . ."

". . . am I telling you this? I don't know, Mr. Sauer. I honestly don't know. I think perhaps I want to feel your contempt. In the back of my mind, I may even have hoped you would shoot me down." He shifted his glance to the window and said reflectively, "A guilty man is a condemned creature, Mr. Sauer. If he is also an honest man, then he is doubly damned because he can find no escape from his guilt in lies and sham. There is no escape for me. I joined that mob six months ago in spite of my training in the law, in spite of the fact that everything I had been taught abhorred mob violence. I joined it in a moment of passion, in a moment of blind fury

99

because I had lost something . . ." His mouth twisted ruefully. ". . . something I'd never even had."

Lane stared at him puzzledly.

Kemmerer waved a hand toward a chair. Lane perched uncomfortably on the edge of it.

Kemmerer asked, "Do you know what sort of woman she was, Mr. Sauer?"

Lane shook his head.

"She was a beautiful woman. A mature woman—no damn flibbertigibbet girl. To the men in love with her she was . . . a saint, I suppose. To those who were having affairs with her, she was an abused and misunderstood wife. Not a one of her lovers would believe he was not the only one."

Lane tried to keep what he was feeling out of his expression. Why, he could not have said. Certainly he owed this man no pity, no concern. He did not even owe him understanding. The judge was no better than Riker was. He was worse, because he knew the evil he did while passion was high and anger hot. Kemmerer could have stopped the mob but he had not. He had joined it instead.

The judge now found it impossible to meet Lane's eyes. "I am the worst of the lot of them. She was not even mine. She had never been mine. I used to sit here in this chair and look down into the street at her and, like some adolescent schoolboy I would think what it would be like if she was mine. I would think that someday she would turn to me and we would go away . . ."

He flushed slowly, darkly. "We would never have gone away because she would never have turned to me. I am an old man. Worse, I am an old fool, or was. I joined the mob and helped hang your brother not because I thought he had killed a woman but because I thought he had killed a dream."

There was a long silence. The judge stared emptily, silently out the window. Lane watched him, angered at himself because he felt pity for the man.

What about Jess? he thought. Who had felt pity for Jess? The law provided penalties for murder. What about Jess's murderers? What penalty would be assessed against Jess's murderers?

The judge turned his head. His face was almost gray now and all life seemed to have fled from his eyes. As though he had been reading Lane's mind, he said, "You are wondering about the penalty for murder such as the men of Saguaro committed against your brother six months ago. Let me tell you something, Mr. Sauer. Not a night of that six months has passed but what I hanged your brother in my dreams and then found out it had been a mistake. Not a night has passed but what I woke up in a cold sweat, crying out into the darkness of my room. . . ."

"You said, 'Some of us might let you go.' What did you mean by that?"

"Just that. Some of us are not willing to commit another murder to hide the first."

"But you won't help. You won't stick your neck out to help. Is that it, Judge?"

Kemmerer concentrated fully on Lane. "What do you want me to do?"

"I don't expect you to shoot it out with the town, if that's what you mean. But I'd like to know, if I'm going to die, that it won't have been for nothing. I'd like to know that word will get out to my family about what happened to Jess and to me." He stared almost defiantly at the judge. "You want to ease your guilt. All right. Get a letter to my family."

He could see that the idea frightened Kemmerer. The judge stared down into the street for a long, long time.

Then he turned his head and stared at Lane's battered face. A moment passed while a look of unutterable self-contempt crossed his face. He said, "God forgive me. After what I've done, I can still worry about what someone like Riker can do to me."

Lane waited. Kemmerer finally said, "They are watching you and they will know that you have been here."

Lane nodded.

"I'll have to tell them something."

"Tell 'em you refused to help me."

The judge shook his head. "That won't jibe with things I said earlier today."

Lane stared unbelievingly at him. He said, "Good God, man, you're the county judge. Tell 'em nothing. Tell 'em to mind their own damn business."

Kemmerer nodded. He said, "Sit down and write the letter. I'll see that it gets to your family."

He got up from his desk. He got paper and an envelope and Lane sat down at the desk. This was the third letter he had written, he thought. He wondered if this one would get through.

He wrote substantially the same letter he had written earlier today and left beneath his plate in the hotel dining room. He finished it, signed it and put it into the envelope. He addressed the envelope carefully and handed it to the judge.

The judge stared down at it, read the address and looked up at Lane. He said, "Tell me about your father. Tell me about your brothers."

"Why?"

"I would like to know what it is in a man that makes him raise sons like your brother and yourself. You know you're going to be killed in a couple of hours or less. Yet you're not afraid. At least you're functioning. You're doing what you can to salvage something, to make your death count. Your brother was the same way. He screamed that he was innocent. He screamed for a fair, honest trial. He cursed the men who intended to murder him, but he never begged, Mr. Sauer. He never begged and he never gave them any other satisfaction. He sat that horse with the noose around his neck and looked right into their eyes. Then he turned his head and spit in his executioner's face. That was when the whip fell. You might say your brother hanged himself. He chose the moment it would happen to him, the moment he would die."

Lane felt an odd and pleasant stir of pride. He wished he had known that, wished he had written it in the letter. He said, "My father settled our ranch when he was twenty-five. He brought my mother with him in a wagon. He had a cow and a bull tied on behind, and my mother had two hens and a rooster in a crate."

Almost blankly he stared at the judge, not really seeing him. He said, "My mother had seven boys, and one little girl that died at birth. She was killed by an Indian arrow when I was fifteen. After that we got along by ourselves."

He said, turning toward the door, "I'll keep 'em occupied, by trying to get on the stage. While I'm doing it, you can get the letter to the stage driver without being seen."

The judge nodded. He hesitated a moment. At last he said, "You can stop worrying about not getting word to your family. Even if this letter does not get out . . . I have the address and I'll see they know the truth about your brother and yourself if I have to take the word to them myself."

Lane murmured his thanks. At least, he thought, he'd found one man willing to take a stand. The judge would try getting the letter out.

That didn't mean, of course, that he'd succeed in doing so. He might die down in the street when the stage came in.

Lane walked along the hall to the outside stairway and descended it. Time was getting short. The stage would be arriving soon. But he had done his best. He'd done everything he could. He could only wait and see what the town would do.

CHAPTER 12

Holt Childers followed Brooks toward the front of the store. He watched the hotel man hurry across the street. Through the front windows of the store he studied the stranger, sitting indolently on the hotel veranda. The man looked relaxed, he thought, in spite of the marks of Riker's fists on his face. But he couldn't be relaxed. It was impossible.

Sauer knew what had happened to his brother six months ago. He knew that, yet he could sit over there as though he hadn't anything better to do, as though he hadn't a care in the world.

Childers frowned. Sauer's indolence was an illusion. It had to be. Beneath his seeming relaxation, he was probably like a coiled steel spring. Prod him and he would react like a rattlesnake.

He turned away, suddenly appalled that he, along with Riker and Brooks, had just cold-bloodedly planned this stranger's death. Then he began to justify himself. Sauer was only one man. Why should he be allowed to wreck a town, to ruin fifty men? It wasn't as if doing so would bring his brother back. Nothing could bring his brother back.

Nor was it as though the men of Saguaro weren't sorry

for what they'd done. They *were* sorry, every one of them. Childers himself would give half of what he owned if it hadn't happened, if Jess Sauer was still alive. But he wasn't alive and Childers didn't intend to give up everything just to satisfy his brother's need for vengeance.

Scowling, he sat down at his roll-top desk, ignoring the papers that littered it. There was no use looking back. What was done was done. He hadn't asked Sauer to come here snooping around and, even if he wanted to, he couldn't stop the other men of the town from getting rid of him. The best thing to do now was to make sure the plan for killing Sauer worked.

The plan's biggest flaw, he thought, was its simplicity. But besides its simplicity, it had another flaw. That flaw was Burt Manus.

Earlier, out at the cemetery, Childers had stopped Manus when it seemed the sheriff was about to force a showdown with Sauer over digging up the grave. He wished he hadn't, now, because since then Manus had apparently had a change of heart. He'd recovered Sauer's gun and money belt. By returning them to him, he'd given Sauer the tools he needed to put up a fight.

Childers' scowl deepened. If Manus was around when the stage came in, he'd interfere. Childers would just have to see to it Manus wasn't around when the stage came in. It was as simple as that. Someone would have to go down to the jail just before stage time and lock the sheriff in one of his own jail cells.

Who? He got up and began to pace back and forth up and down the long aisle. It would have to be someone Manus believed capable of shooting him or he'd simply laugh at the threat. It had to be someone who had a lot to lose if Sauer got away. Harris Gentry, he thought. Gentry was the perfect choice. Knowing Gentry's war record,

Manus wouldn't question any threat Gentry made. He'd surrender his gun and meekly let himself be herded into a cell.

Childers strode decisively out the front door of his store. He wheeled sharply left and climbed the outside stairway leading to the offices over the furniture store.

Gentry's office was the first one on the right. He went in without knocking. Gentry had his chair swiveled around and was staring out the window into the street.

He swung his head jerkily as Childers came in but relaxed immediately when he saw who it was. Childers closed the door behind him and said, "We've got a plan, Harris, but we need your help."

Wariness instantly touched Gentry's eyes. Childers said quickly, "It's nothing to do with . . . well . . . with actually killing him. But it's an important part of the plan."

Gentry straightened in his chair. He didn't speak.

Childers said, "It's Manus. We've got it planned so that Sauer will be killed in a street fight when the stage comes in. Only we've got to be sure Manus isn't there to interfere. He recovered Sauer's gun and money belt. That means he intends to let Sauer get on the stage and get away."

Gentry said, "Why don't you *let* him, then? There could be a stage holdup half a dozen miles out of town, couldn't there? Sauer could get shot."

"I thought of that but it's too risky. Len Miller's liable to shoot back. He might recognize someone, even if they did use masks. And there's that whisky drummer, Meyer. He'll be on the stage."

Gentry nodded. "All right. What do you want me to do?"

"Watch for the stage to come into sight up on the ridge. When you see it, go down to Manus' office. Shove a gun in his back and herd him into one of the cells. He won't put up a fight with you. He knows you'll do just what you say you will."

"All right."

"Keep him there until you hear shots up here in front of the hotel. Then you can turn him loose."

Gentry frowned. "How's this going to help? All we're doing is getting rid of this one man. Others in his family will come to see what happened to him."

Childers nodded. "Sure. But when they're told he was killed in a street fight . . . well, maybe they won't look too closely into the disappearance of the other one."

"What if they do?"

An irritated expression touched Holt Childers' face. He said impatiently, "What if they do? Good God Almighty, I can't think of everything! We're doing the best we can, that's all. Maybe it isn't perfect but it's the best we can come up with right now. If we let this man get away, he's going to spread the news of that lynching all over the country, from San Francisco to St. Louis. There'll be big-city newspapermen here, writing stories, looking for interviews. They'll ruin your reputation and mine and that of everyone else in town. They'll make a Roman holiday out of it. All I'm doing now is preventing that. I can't look into the future and say what will happen a month from now. So don't sit there and tell me what *might* happen. I'm trying to stop what I know *will* happen if I don't do something today."

Gentry nodded. His expression was abashed, startled at Childers' show of temper. He said, "I'll take care of Burt."

Childers studied him closely for several moments. Then, apparently satisfied, he nodded and turned back to the door. He went out.

Gentry listened to his heavy steps on the outside stairway. Looking down from his window he saw Childers appear on the walk, turn and go into his store.

He frowned, trying to understand himself. He guessed that, in a sense, he was fighting for his life. All his instincts of self-preservation had come into play. He was willing to do, today, what six months ago would have seemed incomprehensible to him. He was prepared to become an accessory to cold-blooded, deliberate murder. It was true that he didn't have to do the dirty work, but it might have been better if he did. Maybe if he had to do the actual killing his stomach would refuse what his conscience had failed to refuse.

He felt a stir of self-revulsion that was almost physical, almost a shudder like one caused by an unexpected glimpse of a rattlesnake. He had thought, during the war, that killing had marked him as terribly as it was possible for a man to be marked.

He had ordered men into action he knew meant certain death for most of them. He had killed men himself with his saber while leading a cavalry charge. He'd had spies and deserters shot. Death had become commonplace, as acceptable a state as life. He had learned its smell, its sweet, sickening smell. At times he had wished he was dead himself because it didn't seem right that he should live while so many others died.

But that had been different from the thing six months ago. During the war he had fought for a cause. Six months ago he had acted from the basest motives a man can have.

He had felt rage . . . no, outrage, to which he had no right. He could not justify his own fury on that terrible night. It had not been fury for wronged womanhood; it had been the fury of personal loss. Not again would he hold Lorina Newkirk in his arms. Not again because she had been killed, brutally, wantonly, unnecessarily by a man she probably had not even refused.

He suddenly felt cold. It was a chill that began somewhere in the pit of his stomach and spread until it seemed to congest his lungs and restrict his heart. He alone of all her lovers had known the truth. He alone had known exactly what Lorina was. And yet, to his everlasting shame, he still had gone back to her. Knowing he was not the only one, he still had gone back.

He could have killed her himself, he thought. Many times he could have killed her himself, so great was his disgust. He hadn't killed her, though, because he had known, even in his moments of disgust, that Lorina was not to blame for what she was. Nor, he supposed, was he to blame because he couldn't stay away from her.

Angrily he got up out of his chair. He kicked the spittoon savagely and it rolled across the floor to bang against the wall with a great clatter.

For a moment he considered what would happen, what actually would happen to him personally if Sauer got out of town safely and spread the news of the lynching six months ago.

Professionally he would be ruined, of course. No attorney who has participated in a lynching could expect to continue to practice law. Political office would likewise be barred to him.

He paced nervously back and forth. He could live, even without the law, even without politics. But could he live without his friends and neighbors here in Saguaro? Could he live with himself knowing that he had betrayed his friends? God knew, murder was bad enough. In Gentry's mind, betrayal was much worse.

He heard footsteps in the hall, and the door of his office opened. He glanced around and saw his wife standing there. She closed the door behind her and came halfway across the room.

She was a tiny woman, frail-appearing. She carried a parasol to shield her head from the direct rays of the sun. There was a slight shine of perspiration on her face that in no way detracted from her ladylike appearance.

Gentry knew her appearance of frailty was deceptive. She was one of the strongest women he had ever known. Her will drove her slight body to tasks that seemed impossible for it. Now she asked firmly, "Harris, I should like to know what is going on."

"Going on?" He wished he didn't feel so much like a small boy when she spoke to him like this.

"Yes, Harris, going on. That man sitting down there on the hotel veranda—he looks a great deal like the one who was . . . who was here six months ago. And he has been beaten up. I must ask that you tell me what is going on."

He knew there was no use evading. Not when she used this tone. He remembered another time when she had used it—on the day after Jess Sauer was hanged.

She had asked him, point-blank, what his connection with Lorina Newkirk had been. He had tried to put her off but she would not be put off. "Was she your mistress, Harris? Were you in love with her?"

He remembered the way she had looked that day, erect, proud, regal, even though she would not directly meet his glance. And when he had admitted his relationship with Lorina he had seen the fleeting look of almost intolerable pain that crossed her face. She had said, "I have suspected it. And now you have helped hang an innocent man because of her. What are you going to do now, Harris? How can I help?"

He had never experienced shame greater than that he

had felt that day. Her loyalty was unwavering, in spite of what he had done. He had betrayed her with Lorina; he had helped commit murder, yet she remained steadfast. All she had asked was how she could help.

Now she stood in the center of his office, her blue eyes fixed steadily on him and repeated, "Harris, I must ask that you tell me what is going on in Saguaro today."

He turned his back to her and stared at Sauer on the hotel veranda across the street. He growled, "Nothing's going on."

"Oh yes there is. That man *is* his brother, isn't he? And he's found out what happened here six months ago. What are the men of the town going to do, Harris? Are they going to kill him too?"

He turned his head. "Go home, Belle. This isn't woman's business."

"Maybe it is woman's business. Maybe what happened six months ago was woman's business. Oh Harris, please. Let me help you. Why must you always be so sure you know so much more than I?"

He said almost angrily, "I can't tell you anything."

"Why? Because you believe doing so would betray your friends? They *are* going to murder that man down there, aren't they? And you're to be a part of it."

"I didn't say that."

"No, I said it. I won't stand for it, Harris. I'll interfere. What happened six months ago was bad enough, but it was, in some ways, understandable. You were caught up in mob hysteria. You thought the man guilty of a terrible crime. But this man has committed no crime. He is not even accused of a crime. All he has done is come here looking for his brother, trying to find out what happened to him."

He looked at her beseechingly, knowing he was no match for her. He said, "Go home, Belle. Please!"

Adamantly she shook her head. "I will be down in the street until I see what happens to that man. I will help him if I can. Don't be a part of killing him, Harris. Don't make yourself a murderer again."

Gentry's face was cold. So was his voice. "Do as you please, Mrs. Gentry. I will do what I believe I have to do."

She stood there studying his face for a long, long time. An expression of defeat touched her eyes. She nodded dumbly, turned and went out the door. He heard her footsteps briefly in the hall, heard the outside door close. He crossed to the window and stared down into the street. He saw her come off the stairs, hesitate on the walk, then turn uptown toward Holt Childers' mercantile store.

He turned his head and lifted his glance to the top of the ridge. It wasn't yet time for the stage to come in. He returned his glance to the street, letting it rest on Sauer's relaxed form on the hotel veranda.

Damn the man! Why had he had to come here? Why hadn't anyone known about the letter Jess Sauer wrote from here and stopped it from going out?

He shrugged and turned away from the window. He sat down behind his desk. Leaning over, he opened the lower right-hand drawer.

There in the drawer was a Colt's pocket pistol that he'd had for years. He picked it up, spun the cylinder and checked the loads. He laid it on the desk, then picked it up and stuck it into his belt. It was uncomfortable there so he withdrew it and dropped it into his side coat pocket, where it made a sagging bulge.

All he could do now was wait, he thought. All he could do was wait.

CHAPTER 13

Jake Newkirk stood behind the bar in his saloon. He reached for a bottle and poured himself a drink although it was not yet eleven o'clock. Over the tops of the swinging doors he could see the hotel veranda across the street and the stranger sitting there. The man had spent the morning there except for once when he had walked across the street.

Meyer came out of the hotel carrying his valise. He put it down, withdrew a handkerchief from his pocket and mopped his brow. He ducked back inside the hotel.

Newkirk turned his head and looked resentfully at his back bar. Meyer had quit coming here on his monthly trips to town, because Jake didn't buy anything from him any more. Meyer knew something was wrong, of course, but he had never mentioned Jake's lack of customers.

Jake gulped his drink and strode angrily to the doors. He stared over their tops into the sun-washed, baking street. He hated this town, he thought. He hated every man in this goddam town. But three of them he hated even more than all the rest. Childers. Gentry. Brooks. Those three had been seeing Lorina while he spent his nights here trying to earn enough to keep her supplied with the pretty things she was always asking for. The bitch! The dirty, lousy bitch! All he had been good for was to keep this saloon going, keep a roof over her head and food on her table. While he was doing that, the "gentlemen" in town, the ones with white shirts and clean hands, had been calling on her.

Gentlemen! He snorted contemptuously to himself. Gentlemen or no, they'd joined the mob and helped hang Jess Sauer for killing her. They'd kept their hands clean, letting others do the actual dirty work, but they'd been there all the same, egging the others on, lending their support to everything that was done.

He left the door and began to pace nervously back and forth. He hadn't known Lorina was unfaithful to him until the next day, until after Jess Sauer was dead. He wouldn't have had a part of lynching him if he *had* known. He wouldn't have helped lynch a man for killing a woman as rotten as Lorina had been.

But the town blamed him, as though the whole thing had been his fault, as though Lorina's evil had been his fault. They blamed him and they stopped coming into his saloon as though he had leprosy or something. He kept it open in spite of the lack of customers but he was about at the end of his rope. The rent was three months past due and Childers, who owned the building, wasn't going to wait much longer for it. He'd have him evicted for non-payment of rent and that would be the end of Newkirk's Emporia saloon.

He was ruined. This town had ruined him—not because of anything he had done, either, but only because he had been Lorina's husband, because he reminded them of her and of what they had done because of her. They wanted to be rid of him. They wanted him broke—so broke he'd have to leave town for good.

He glanced up surprisedly as Otto Riker came through

the swinging doors. Riker strode heavily across to the bar, removed his hat and ran the hairy back of a hand across his streaming brow. He said, "Whisky, Jake."

Newkirk slid him a bottle and a glass. Riker said, "Look at the son of a bitch, sittin' over there, daring the town to do somethin' to him. Well, I'll tell you somethin', Jake. He ain't got long to wait. When the stage comes in, I'm goin' over there an' take the bastard apart, piece by piece."

Newkirk didn't reply. He wondered why Riker had suddenly come in for a drink today. It was the first time Riker had been in since the lynching six months before.

Riker wanted something from him, he thought. He wanted his support, or his help, or something. Riker hadn't just come in to buy a drink.

Jake hadn't talked to anybody about the stranger but he knew who he was. You couldn't miss it, he looked so much like the other one, the one they'd hanged.

He stared resentfully at Riker. "You son of a bitch, I hope he takes *you* apart. If you came in here to get me to help, you can forget it. You and every other bastard in this town that has stayed out of here for six months can forget about asking me to help do anything. I hope he gets away. I hope he tells the whole damn world what was done in this town six months ago. I hope he brings an army back and gets revenge against the lot of you."

"You helped, Jake. You talked us into it. He'll be after you just like he'll be after the rest of us."

"Will he? I doubt it. Remember, I had more justification than anyone. She was my wife, even if she was a bitch. What have I got to lose if he ruins this stinkin' town? My business? My saloon? Hell, it's already lost. There isn't enough stock in here to pay the rent that's overdue. This damned town has ruined me. And why? Because I led that mob? Or because every time they look at me they remember what it was like that night, because when some of them look at me they know I know what was goin' on between them and my wife. That's why they haven't been coming here."

Riker scowled blackly at him. He finished his drink and slammed a coin down on the bar. He said truculently, "You get this through your head, Jake. Don't interfere. Don't stick your big nose into it when that stage comes in. We're going to get rid of that bastard and if you get in the way we'll get rid of you too."

Jake laughed harshly. "Big talk! You'll be doing good if you get rid of him. He's got his gun back now. And he can outdraw you any day of the week."

"He won't draw against an unarmed man. If he does . . ."

Jake stared at the blacksmith, hostility in his eyes. "Yeah. If he does, you'll have somebody planted to shoot him down. Is that it? Is that what you wanted from me, to stand here in my doorway with a rifle ready to shoot him if he draws his gun? Go to hell, you son of a bitch! Get somebody else to do your dirty work."

Riker glowered at him furiously for several moments. His face was red, congested with blood. His eyes were narrowed, tiny and murderous. But Newkirk's glance didn't falter and at last Riker turned and lumbered angrily out into the street.

Jake stared at the doors, swinging back and forth. Riker must be worse-scared of the stranger than he was willing to admit, he thought. Otherwise, he wouldn't have bothered to ask him to stand ready here with a gun. Why did he need to ask him anyway? Riker and Murphy were thick as thieves. How come Murphy wasn't covering for Riker today?

He scowled. Murphy probably was, he thought. Riker

just wanted extra insurance. He was really counting on Murphy to shoot the stranger down if he touched his gun.

He walked back to the bar. Automatically he returned the bottle he had shoved at Riker to its place and automatically washed the glass.

Frowning, staring out over the tops of the doors but not really seeing anything, he found himself remembering how it had been that night six months ago. He hadn't known what kind of woman Lorina was. Maybe he'd been both stupid and blind, but he hadn't known. All he'd known that night was that someone had murdered her and left her ravished body lying in the alley behind their house.

Manus found the stranger heading out across the desert half an hour after Lorina's body was found. He captured him and brought him back to jail.

Newkirk remembered the way he, himself, had been. Numb. Shocked and unbelieving. When Harry Zeeb drew back the sheet covering her and he saw her lying there . . .

In spite of the heat of the day, he suddenly felt cold. It was as though he was standing there looking down at her again. He'd seen her body, her battered face in his dreams a hundred times since then. He'd wakened each time, bathed with sweat, his hands closed around the bedpost as though it was the killer's throat.

He remembered only vaguely leaving Zeeb's store and staggering down the street to the saloon. He remembered the noise in the saloon, and the way it hushed when he came in. He remembered the raw taste of whisky in his throat as he drank to try to forget that she was dead.

He had loved her. God help him, he had loved her and he hadn't known she was seeing other men. He hadn't known that until the next day.

The more he drank that night, the clearer everything

seemed in his mind. He remembered someone running into the saloon yelling that Manus had brought the killer in. The "killer," the man had said. Not "a suspect," but "the killer." After that there had been a lot of yelling and milling around. He remembered doing a lot of yelling himself, with tears streaming down his face all the while. It had never occurred to him to doubt that the captured man was the guilty one. In his state of grief and shock it had never occurred to him to doubt. And he'd felt he owed it to Lorina to see that retribution overtook her killer immediately. Only when her killer was dead could he find peace within his tortured mind.

So he led the mob, a great, numbed man with tears streaming down his face, he had led the mob. He had shut his ears to Jess Sauer's protestations of innocence, to his demands for a fair, impartial trial. And the next day he found out the truth.

That Sauer was innocent. And that Lorina wasn't what he had thought she was.

In a way, he couldn't blame the men for avoiding his saloon in the days that followed the lynching. He hadn't been what a person would consider good company. He'd honestly thought he was going out of his mind. It was bad enough to grieve for someone you have loved. It was worse to grieve for the virtue that a loved one had never even possessed. Worst of all was grieving for a murdered man, the innocent victim of a town's blind rage.

But they *had* boycotted him. They *had* blamed him for leading them. They *had* let him go broke because just the sight of him renewed their own intolerable feelings of guilt.

Now they wanted to kill another man, a man as innocent as the first. The only crime this man was guilty of was searching for his brother. Riker had beaten him up last night. Today Riker meant to kill him, or have him killed, and the whole town would stand by and watch. The whole town would approve.

Jake wondered if Burt Manus knew what was going on. Probably, he thought. But he might not have guessed the details of the plan.

He wondered, briefly, if Burt Manus was in on it. That was something he couldn't know until he had talked to Burt. Abruptly he removed his apron and strode to the door.

Coming out into the bright sunlight, he blinked almost owlishly. He raised a hand and ran it across his whiskered face. He combed his hair with his fingers. He'd been getting careless lately, he thought. He seldom shaved and he didn't often take a bath. He guessed he just didn't care. He looked down at his rumpled, dirty clothes. This was what a woman could do to a man, he thought. She just plain took the heart out of him. She made a fool of him, shamed him before his friends and before himself. She took away his pride.

Resolutely, he strode down the street toward the jail. The front door was open and he went in. It was cooler inside and there was the light smell of disinfectant that Manus used to clean the cells in the rear. Manus was sitting at his desk, scowling almost angrily. He looked at Newkirk and his face softened as though he was seeing Jake, really seeing him for the first time in many months. He nodded. "Hello, Jake. What brings you down here?"

Jake made up his mind right then that he was through letting the town beat him. He was through letting himself run down like an old man who didn't care. There were other towns to which he could go. He'd started here with nothing and he could start someplace else the same way. Only this time there wouldn't be any Lorina weighting him down, taking everything he had to give and more. In time . . . hell, in time he might even meet another woman. He was only forty-five years old.

He said, "Burt, there's something going on that you ought to know about. Riker's going to jump that stranger when the stage comes in."

"Sauer's got a gun. I doubt if Riker can beat him to the draw."

"He won't have to. Riker isn't going to have a gun, but when he threatens the stranger, Sauer's sure to grab his. As quick as he does I figure somebody's going to cut him down."

Manus straightened in his chair. "You know this for sure?"

Jake shook his head. "Not for sure. I'm guessing part of it. But Riker was in my saloon a few minutes ago fishing around and he hasn't been in there for months. He wanted me to be ready with a gun. I told him to go to hell."

Manus nodded. "Thanks for telling me. I'll take a walk up there when I see the stage at the top of the ridge."

Jake nodded. He hesitated a moment. Then, without another word, he went out and walked up the street toward his saloon. The first thing he was going to do was wash and shave. After that, he was going to see Childers and find out what he could salvage out of the saloon.

Inside his saloon, he removed his shirt. He went out back to the pump and filled a basin. He washed, shaved and combed his hair. He came back in and put on his shirt again.

He took two quick drinks because nervousness was beginning in him now. Then he went out and walked up the street toward Holt Childers' mercantile.

He hated to ask any favors of Holt, because Holt had

been one of his wife's "friends." But it was to Childers that he owed the rent. He had to settle with him.

Childers was standing near the front of his store, staring at the stranger across the street. Jake Newkirk said, "I've got to talk to you. I owe you three months' rent, but I've got some stock and I've got some furniture. I want to leave town and I want to know what you'll give me and take over the whole damn thing."

Childers looked at him. He said, "I'll talk to you later about it. I'm busy now."

Jake clenched his fists. He said, "You talk to me about it now. I want to leave this stinkin' town. I want to know how much you'll give me for my saloon."

Childers frowned, but his mind was still not fully on what Jake had said. He said, "I won't give you anything, but I'll take it over for the rent."

Jake stared at him a moment. Childers was still watching the stranger sitting on the veranda across the street. There was a look almost like fascination on his face.

Jake wanted to hit Childers in the mouth. He clenched his fist. He thought about it and decided he'd better not. He still might get enough to pay his stage fare from some-one else.

Sourly he turned and went outside. He hated Childers even more than he had before. But now he hated himself as well. He should have some pride, he thought. He should fight back against this lousy town. He should have killed all three of his wife's lovers six months ago, as soon as he found out about them. Damn them, they were all alike. They were all like Childers had been a few minutes ago. They looked down their noses at a man like they were better than he was. But they didn't mind sneaking around with his wife behind his back.

He reached his saloon and went inside. He poured himself a drink and gulped it down. He poured another and gulped that down.

He kept pouring and drinking and with each drink his anger and frustration increased. Childers and the others had made a fool of him. They'd taken his wife and they'd ruined his business. They even had the gall to blame him for that stranger's death six months ago.

What he should do now was what he should have done six months ago. Make them pay. Blow the goddam brains out of all three of them. They just hadn't better push him any more. Nobody had better push him any more.

Scowling, he stared out into the street.

CHAPTER 14

Nicolo Finch rolled out of his bunk at dawn. He sat on the edge of it for a moment, staring at the floor between his feet. He had lain awake almost the whole night, thinking about the stranger who had come in on the stagecoach yesterday, thinking back to the hanging of the other one six months before. He didn't know what Lane Sauer knew about his brother's death but he had sure as hell come to the right place to find out.

And when he did find out . . . That was what had kept Finch from sleeping last night. He knew what the people of Saguaro would do to Sauer if he happened to discover their guilty secret.

He got up and pulled on his pants and shirt. He strapped on his gunbelt and shoved the gun into its holster. He walked to the door of the bunkhouse and stepped outside.

It was already hot, but this was not the heat of the desert floor. At this altitude, it never got as hot as it did in the town of Saguaro. Up here, there was a light rain almost every afternoon. A stream wound down the valley, irrigating the hay and providing water for the stock.

Only in winter did the cattle ever stray down onto the desert floor, only when snow covered the grass up here. It was on one such day last winter, the day after the hanging, that he and another man had come upon the killer of Lorina Newkirk out on the desert while looking for strays.

Finch walked toward the house, a rambling, one-story adobe building with a walled courtyard. He met John Smitherman coming out and asked, "Reckon I could have the day off today?"

Smitherman nodded, studying Finch with a light frown. "Something the matter? Anything I can do?"

Finch shook his head. "I can take care of it." He had been in town the day of the hanging, but he'd never told Smitherman about it. He'd never told anyone and never would. It wasn't the kind of thing a man could talk about. It lay in his mind and heart, a deep shame that might trouble him less as time passed but which would never entirely go away.

He got a horse out of the corral, saddled and mounted and rode out as the sun poked above the horizon in the east. It was a long ride into town, almost thirty miles. He couldn't make it much before noon no matter how he tried. But he had to try. He felt a responsibility. He wished now he had talked to Sauer yesterday on the long stage ride.

Although Nicolo didn't think of it that way, his own innate decency had gotten him involved in the first place. He was a lonely man who had spent his life riding after cattle in isolated places like this. If he got to town twice a year, it was a lot.

Living this way, he had very little to do with women and little contact with them. He thought of Mary Smitherman, the boss's wife, the way he had thought of his mother before she died—with deep respect that amounted almost to reverence. She was the only "good" woman he knew. The others . . .

In Finch's world there were two kinds of women and

only two. The good and bad. Consequently, when he had seen the body of Lorina Newkirk brought in to the undertaker's establishment, he had been thoroughly enraged. A good woman of the town had been subjected to treatment the bad ones didn't even deserve. Some man-turned-animal had crossed the line separating decency from savagery and had killed something good and fine. The man deserved to die. He deserved no mercy, no pity at all.

The possible innocence of Jess Sauer never occurred to Nicolo. His guilt had seemed cut and dried. Burt Manus had arrested him and had brought him back to town. Sauer had scratches on his face. He had been seen watching Lorina in the hotel dining room. Nobody had seen any other strangers in town that day.

Besides, Judge Kemmerer had held a trial. Not a regular trial, he supposed, because it had been held at night and in the open down by the cottonwood, but a trial where the man's guilt had been decided upon.

That was, at least, how it seemed that night. The next day everything looked different. The next day all Nicolo could think was that a man just like himself had died at the hands of a mob for something he hadn't even done. And that he, himself, had been part of the mob. It had been his horse the man had sat upon.

He wondered what the town would do to Sauer. He supposed it would depend on what Sauer did, or threatened to do to the town. Finch wouldn't have blamed Sauer if he sought vengeance against every man involved.

He touched his horse's sides with his spurs. The animal broke into a lope. Just as well cover as much distance as possible while it still was cool, Finch thought.

Ten miles from the ranch, he struck the stage road, and thereafter followed that on into town. It was a little after eleven when he arrived.

The town looked sleepy, like it always did. As Finch came down River Street toward the hotel, he saw Sauer leave the hotel veranda and head for the furniture store across the street.

Seeing Sauer gave him a sudden, almost overwhelming feeling of relief. He grinned ruefully to himself. He didn't know what he'd expected, but he was glad to see Sauer was still alive. He drew his horse to a halt briefly in front of the hotel, then rode on, halting in front of Newkirk's saloon. He dismounted and tied his horse.

Sauer came out of the furniture store carrying a white grave marker. He turned the corner and disappeared in the direction of the cemetery.

Nicolo frowned. Sauer knew, then. He knew his brother had been lynched. He studied the street suddenly. Sleepy wasn't exactly the word for it. Empty would fit it better. Ominously empty. At this time of day there should be women in the street, and children, and men going back and forth. At this moment not a man, woman or child was visible.

Finch went into the saloon. Newkirk was behind the bar, scowling. Finch said, "He knows what happened, doesn't he?"

Newkirk nodded.

Finch said, "My guess is he's going to need some help."

Newkirk nodded. "Riker's fixin' to jump him when he tries to get on the stage. I figure Murphy will be waiting in his shop in case he goes for his gun."

"The sheriff know this?"

Newkirk nodded. "I went down and told him a little while ago."

"Then he'll take care of it."

Jake nodded. "Unless he'd rather see Sauer dead."

Finch said, "I got in that thing six months ago because

127

of your wife being such a fine woman and all, but this man isn't accused of doing anything. I guess if they jump him . . . well, I'll just have to help him out."

Newkirk's laugh was bitter, harsh. He started to say something, then suddenly and unaccountably closed his mouth. He said, "Yeah. You help him out."

Finch looked at him strangely, but he didn't speak. He finished his drink and laid a coin down on the bar. He went out, crossed the street to the hotel and sat down on the veranda in the chair Sauer had just vacated. He put his feet up on the rail and rolled himself a cigarette.

Lane Sauer had not expected the marker to be ready when he called for it. But it was ready, and the date was there: January 9, 1871. He paid for it and, careful not to smudge the paint, carried it out the door and turned the corner toward the cemetery.

He didn't know which of the two graves belonged to his brother, so he turned in at the Vargas house and knocked. The girl, Saralee, answered the door, her face pale, her eyes still scared. He said, "I've got a marker for Jess's grave but I don't know which of the two it is. Can you tell me?"

She frowned faintly as though trying to recall. At last she said, "It's the one closest to the river."

"Thanks." He nodded, and turned away. She called after him, "They're not going to let you leave. You know that, don't you?"

He turned his head and nodded. "I know." He stared at her briefly, then turned again and headed for the cemetery. He walked slowly, deliberately, carrying the wooden cross in his left hand.

There was tension in him. There was pain from his broken ribs and from the bruises Riker had given him the night before. He tried to walk without showing either the tension or the pain.

If a man was going to die, and knew it, he ought to be able to do it with a little dignity. Not limping and wincing and acting jumpy. He could die the way Jess had: cursing his killers, not giving them the satisfaction of knowing he was afraid.

He reached the edge of the cemetery. The sun was blazing down now from its zenith overhead. It was almost noon, he guessed. The stage would be in soon.

He walked to Jess's grave. It was the one he had partially dug up earlier in the day. The earth was loose in it and he had no trouble pushing the white cross into the ground. He stood back then, removed his hat and looked somberly at the grave. He tried to call to mind Jess's face as he'd known it back home. Strangely, all he could see was Jess sitting on a horse, his hands tied behind him, a hangman's noose around his neck and Jess's contorted features as he spit squarely into his executioner's face.

Lane felt himself swaying in the awful heat. He shook his head angrily to clear it. He had been seeing things just then. In another moment he'd have seen the executioner's face. Thinking of that gave him a chill. He wondered whose face it would have been.

He pulled his mind back to the present. He bowed his head and closed his eyes, trying hard to remember words he had heard spoken over graves. He said, "The Lord giveth and the Lord taketh away. Ashes to ashes and dust to dust." He opened his eyes, groping for more words, knowing they wouldn't come. He said, "Good-bye, Jess. I may be in the ground alongside of you come night. But maybe this time the word'll get out about it. Maybe this time they won't get away with it."

The silence here in the cemetery was complete. Lane

put his hat on and turned back toward the town. Rising heat waves made things shimmer before his eyes. He felt dizzy and weak. He staggered across the barren, baking ground of the cemetery.

He walked as far as the Vargas house, then stopped again. He went up the packed-dirt walk, but he did not have to knock. The door opened. Saralee stood in the doorway looking at him with a strangely unreadable expression on her face. He said, "I'd like to talk to your father. There are things I have to know."

She nodded and stood aside. He went into the small adobe house.

It was cooler than anyplace he had yet been today. He removed his hat and wiped his forehead with the back of his hand. Saralee said, "Sit down. I will get my father for you."

He nodded and sank into a leather-covered chair. He looked around the room.

There was little of the Spanish here. The floor was of the puncheon type, covered with colorful, hand-woven rugs. The furniture was heavy, handmade furniture of the kind that Lane was used to back home. He could hear Saralee's voice somewhere in the house, speaking softly and urgently. He could not make out her words, but her tone was easily understood. In it he heard patience, understanding, even pity. But he also heard determination.

It seemed a long time before Saralee returned. When she did, she remained in the doorway, studying him. He regarded her steadily, unblinkingly, until her face began to flush. She came on into the room and Vargas appeared behind her, staggering, his face slack, his eyes dull. He saw Lane and winced visibly, afterward refusing to meet his eyes.

Lane said, "There are things I have to know about that

night six months ago. Will you answer some questions for me?"

Vargas nodded without looking at him. He staggered to a chair and fell into it heavily. He licked his lips, leaned forward and put his face down into his hands.

Lane didn't really know how to begin. He supposed the best way was to work back from the actual hanging. The first name he wanted, anyway, was that of the executioner, the one who had held the whip.

He asked, "Who held the whip? Who whipped the horse out from under him?"

CHAPTER 15

It seemed like a long time before Vargas spoke. Then he said a single word, and spoke it like a curse. "Riker."

No surprise touched Lane. He supposed he had expected it. Serving as executioner took a certain kind of man, one who gained stature in his own mind by doing things other men refused to do or were afraid to do.

Lane could understand the hatred in Riker, knowing this. Jess had spit in Riker's face and forced him to bring the whip slashing down, its timing decided by Jess and not by Riker, who would undoubtedly have withheld it longer so that he could enjoy the power its possession gave to him.

Lane could guess how the town must have treated Riker afterward—the same way they had treated Newkirk, probably. They'd have boycotted Riker just as they had Newkirk except for the fact that he owned the only livery stable in town. They had to do business with him.

Even so, Lane was willing to bet there had been unmistakable rejection of Riker as a member of the community. His mouth twisted briefly with contempt for the town's hypocrisy. They'd use Riker. They'd let him serve as executioner for Jess. They'd let him do as he pleased with Lane, and even be glad if he succeeded in killing him. But they'd reject him for doing it. By so rejecting him they could pretend their own hands were not as soiled as his.

Lane nodded. He asked, "Who put the noose around his neck?"

"Murphy."

That didn't surprise Lane either. It explained the closeness between Riker and the gunsmith.

He asked, "Who led the mob? Who started it?"

Severo Vargas looked up at him. There was genuine puzzlement in his face now. He said, "Jake Newkirk led it, but who started it, I couldn't say. Who knows how a mob starts, *señor*? Maybe Jake started it when he came back from seeing her body in the back room of the furniture store. There were tears streaming down his face and he was sobbing like a little child. Someone came in yelling that Manus had caught the killer, that he had him down at the jail."

Lane said harshly, "Think! I want to know what was said after the man yelled that Manus had caught the killer."

Severo frowned. His eyes were vague and he plainly had trouble forcing his mind to remember, to concentrate. Lane asked, "Did Newkirk speak?"

Severo shook his head. "He was weeping. He couldn't speak. It was Childers who stood up and yelled at everybody. He yelled that if we didn't do something about it we had no right to call ourselves men. He said it could have happened to anyone, to his own wife, to Gentry's wife, or to Saralee. He said it was up to us to show every drifter that came through Saguaro that our women were to be let alone."

Lane nodded. He stared at Severo. He wanted to know what Vargas' part had been, but he did not ask. He got to his feet and went to the door. "Thanks. I'm going to take the stage out of here at noon. I had to know those things before I left."

Saralee smiled wanly at him. She said, "Newkirk and Childers and Murphy and Riker could not have made a mob. It took every man in town."

He nodded. She said, "They will not let you leave. They will kill you in the street before they let you get on the stage."

He said, "They'll try." He went out and closed the door behind him. He stood on the gallery for a moment, the heat striking him like a blow. Tension, sleeplessness, not enough food and the beating he'd taken last night had claimed their toll of his strength. By sheer will he forced himself to straighten up, to walk stiffly back to the hotel. He went into the lobby, noticing the cowboy who'd ridden in on the stage with him yesterday sitting on the veranda. The man looked as though he was about to speak, but apparently changed his mind.

Lane climbed the stairs to his room. He unlocked the door, picked up his bag and put it on the bed. He put into it his razor, shaving brush and soap, and the dirty shirt he'd taken off yesterday. He closed the bag.

The tension in him now seemed almost unbearable. When would they make their move, he wondered, and how? Would they simply cut loose on him from ambush, or would one of them take it upon himself to do the dirty work? He'd have to wait and see. He'd have to be ready for whatever they tried to do.

Carrying his bag, he left the room, closing the door behind him. He went slowly down the stairs, crossed to the desk and dropped his key on it. He said, "I'm leaving. How much do I owe?"

"A dollar and a quarter, Mr. Sauer. I hope—" Brooks

broke off the automatic ritual. Sauer knew he'd been about to say, "I hope you had a pleasant stay." He grunted wryly at the man. "Doesn't apply in my case, does it?"

Brooks's face flushed painfully. Lane couldn't resist needling him. He asked, "How will they do it, Mr. Brooks? From ambush? Will it be more than one, or is one enough to carry all the guilt today?"

Brooks's face lost all its color and turned a pasty gray. He didn't reply and Lane asked, "What's the matter, Mr. Brooks?"

Brooks mumbled something and turned away from the desk. He scurried almost frantically into his office. Lane picked up his bag and walked across the lobby to the door.

He was surprised at himself. He'd always thought that when the time came for facing death he would be terrified. He'd thought it would take all the courage he had to face it like a man.

He discovered that wasn't true at all. He knew he would face death when the stage came in but the strange part of it was, he was actually looking forward to it. He was looking forward to finding out who, of all the men in town, had the courage to step forward openly and try to gun him down.

Yet there was another factor involved in the way he felt. Soon, in less than half an hour perhaps, he was going to have his vengeance. When they opened up on him he'd have a chance to shoot back. Even if they killed him, he'd get some of them before he fell.

He sat down in a leather-covered chair close beside the door. He stared eagerly through it into the street. It was almost time. It was almost time for Saguaro to pay up, partially at least, for Jess Sauer's death six months before.

Saralee Vargas stood in the window after Lane had left, watching him go up the street. There was stiffness about his back and in the way he held himself that revealed to her the pain he was suffering. She remembered the tired way his eyes had looked, the tense way he had held his mouth.

He went out of sight and she turned away from the window, her face soft, a hint of moisture in her eyes. It wasn't right that he should have to suffer at the hands of the people of this town. He'd done nothing but come here searching for his brother.

But he was going to die for coming here if something wasn't done. She stared at her father, still sitting in the chair, still with his face buried in his hands.

She could feel pity for him even while she censured him. But she knew suddenly that she was not going to go on indefinitely as she had the past six months. Severo would drink himself to death if something wasn't changed. Or he'd drown in the river, or be trampled by a horse crossing the street, or pass out in the sun and die of the combination of desert heat and alcohol.

He could stop drinking again, as he had once before. But he couldn't as long as he stayed here, as long as he was constantly reminded of what he'd done. He had to get away.

She said unexpectedly, "Father, we're going to take the stage at noon. I'll go pack."

That brought his head up. He stared at her uncomprehendingly. "Leave Saguaro? How can we leave? Everything we own is here."

"We can take a change of clothes and go. We can live, no matter where we are."

Fear came into his eyes. He licked his lips. "They'll

136

kill us, along with him. They'll say I told him about his brother and they'll kill us both for it."

"Nobody's going to get killed." She spoke to him soothingly, as though to a child.

"You don't know that! I say they'll kill us both, right along with him!"

She looked long and steadily at him. "Would that be so bad?" she asked quietly. "Would dying be so terrible? Are you happy with the way you have been living these last six months?"

"What do you mean, am I happy with it? I'm alive. If we try and get on that stage, I'll be dead. They'll kill me just like they'll kill him! And maybe you!"

Saralee said softly, "There are lots of ways of dying, Father. I think maybe that dying from a bullet wound is the easiest of all of them."

"What do you know about it?"

"As much as you, Father."

He dropped his head into his hands again. Saralee stared at him for several moments. Then she turned briskly and went into the bedroom. She began to pack a small valise with the things she valued most and with the necessary clothing for a trip.

She finished and snapped the bag shut. She went into her father's room and packed another small carpetbag. After that she went into the kitchen and got a hoard of gold coins from a can on one of the cupboard shelves.

Her father hadn't moved. She sat down across from him. "I'm going, Father. Are you going with me, or are you going to stay?"

He raised his head. A hint of anger was in his eyes. At least, she thought, he was feeling something besides despair and fear. Anger was a start. He said, "You're chasing after him like a damned Jezebel. You're not thinking

137

about me, you're thinking about him—and about yourself."

She smiled faintly. "And what is so wrong with that? You're a grown man and able to care for yourself. It is time I had a husband and a family of my own."

"You can find a likelier prospect than him. He ain't going to live past noon."

"If he does not, then neither will I live past noon." She reached into her handbag and touched the rusty pistol she had put into it.

He said surlily, "I ain't goin'. I'm stayin' here. Nothin' can make me go."

Saralee stood up. Anger blazed from her eyes. Her voice was tight with it. She said furiously, "Well, I'm going, Father, whether you go or not. If he tries to get on that stage by himself, he won't have a chance. If I am there, and you are, then they'll be afraid to just kill him in the street. And they'll be afraid to come after the coach and fake a robbery."

"What makes you think they'll be afraid? They're not going to let anyone out of Saguaro who might talk about what happened here six months ago."

Saralee turned and walked to the window. She stared out into the baking street. He might be right. Whoever had been selected to kill Lane Sauer might kill her and Severo too. Yet she couldn't believe that every man in town would countenance more murder to hide the murder that had been committed six months ago. There must be enough decency in most of them to stop it before it went any further.

Decency perhaps, she reflected; but stopping a killing today would require more than decency. It would require courage, and planning, and foresight as well. To stop what might happen today the men of the town would first have to know what was going to happen and when.

Saralee went to the window and sat down close to it, facing the bluff behind the town where the stagecoach would appear. She watched steadily for the telltale cloud of dust she knew she would see first.

She could imagine the desperation, the terror in her father now, but she didn't turn her head. This was a battle he would have to fight all by himself. Win or lose, no one could fight it for him.

She thought of Lane Sauer. She had been attracted to him from the moment she first saw him. It was quite possible that her decision to leave Saguaro was influenced, partly at least, by her feeling for Lane. Yet she knew her father was right. In spite of anything she did or didn't do, Lane Sauer wouldn't live past noon. Enough of the men in town wanted him dead so that he wouldn't have a chance, even with help from others in the town.

She made herself one promise as she sat there staring up at the bluff. If Lane was killed today, and if she was not, then she would make it a point to get out of Saguaro some way, some time. She would see to it that the world knew what had happened to Sauer's brother here six months ago.

She might not be able to stop them from killing him. But she could make sure that he hadn't died in vain.

CHAPTER 16

At quarter of twelve by the lobby clock, Lane got stiffly to his feet. Carrying his bag, he went out, crossed the hotel veranda and stepped down onto the walk. He went next door to the combined stage-line office and post office.

Batterton was no longer behind the post-office grille. He was behind another grille above which hung a sign reading "Saguaro and Albuquerque Stage Line."

Meyer was standing in front of it. Lane stepped up behind him and Meyer glanced around. Immediately his face lost color and his hands began to shake. He finished paying for his ticket and sidled away. He hurried through the door and disappeared. Lane said, "Ticket to Albuquerque. That's as far as the line goes, isn't it?"

Batterton nodded without looking up. He reached for a ticket and began to write on it. He stamped it and pushed it beneath the grille.

Lane shoved a twenty-dollar gold piece back to him. Batterton made change silently. His hands were shaking and he nearly dropped the change. Lane scooped it up and dropped it into his pocket. He picked up the ticket and turned to the door.

He walked back to the hotel, pausing only long enough on the veranda to glance up at the ridge where the stage would first appear. He saw nothing, so he went into the hotel and sat down in the chair he had just vacated. He packed and lighted his pipe thoughtfully and deliberately.

Batterton appeared from the direction of the post office next door and glanced at the hotel. Head down, he scurried across to Childers' store. He was inside for no more than a couple of minutes before he reappeared again. He came back across the street and disappeared into the post office.

They all ran to Childers, Lane thought, with everything that happened.

Glancing up, he saw Judge Kemmerer standing at the window of his office looking down into the street. A couple of windows away, he saw another man he did not recognize, also looking out. He frowned to himself as he tried to read the sign on the window over the second man's head. The man moved from behind it and Lane was able to read, "Harris Gentry, Atty. at Law."

Another lawyer, he thought. Another who had been involved in the hanging of Jess six months ago, watching the street now, waiting for the stage to come in and for him to be killed.

He shifted his position and withdrew his gun from its holster. He checked the loads in it and absently spun the cylinder. In his mind he faced the possibility that he wouldn't even get off a shot. The first bullet fired at him might hit a vital spot and drop him in his tracks.

He returned the gun to its holster. He wished he knew how it would start, from what direction the attack would come. He didn't even know who he had to watch.

He glanced down the street toward the sheriff's office. Manus had tried to explain his mistake, the error in judgment that had made the lynching of Jess possible. But where was he now, when he had a chance to redeem that

141

past mistake by preventing another murder intended to conceal the first? Would he close his eyes to this one too, and fail to make an arrest for it? Lane supposed he would. If the story of Jess's death got out, Manus would be finished as a law-enforcement officer. No town in the territory would give him a job, not even as town marshal. As for getting elected sheriff again . . . it would be impossible.

He glanced at the lobby clock again. Nine minutes before twelve. The stage ought to be appearing at any moment now. Lane stared at his hands as he tapped the pipe against the heel of his left hand to empty it. Both hands were shaking. He put the pipe away and clenched his fists. He was scared, he realized. He was alone and about to be attacked and he was scared.

He forced himself to think of home, to imagine what his father and brothers would be doing now. He stared unseeingly out into the street.

He was scared, but the people of Saguaro were also scared. They were, maybe, more frightened than he. They had begun to pay for what they had done to Jess, and no matter what happened when the stage came in, they would continue to pay. Someone in Saguaro would get word to his family—Saralee, or Kemmerer, or someone else. His father and brothers would come here and know he'd tried, and between them they'd do what he hadn't been able to do alone.

He felt his fear beginning to evaporate, to be replaced by a kind of fatalism. It did no good to be afraid. Fear was the natural function that kept a man from getting himself into danger. He was already in this, with no way of getting out save for the way he'd already decided upon. The time for fear was past. It would all be over in a half hour and when it was he would either be alive or dead. Which, he supposed, depended almost entirely upon himself.

Gentry knew Lane had called on Kemmerer this morning. He could guess what had been discussed. Sauer was getting desperate. He had tried to post two letters and had failed both times. He was beginning to see the handwriting on the wall. He knew he might die when the stage got in and he was trying desperately to get word out to his family.

With the gun a heavy weight in his side coat pocket, Gentry got up from his desk and went to the door. He opened it and walked silently along the hall to Kemmerer's office door. Without knocking, he opened it.

Judge Kemmerer, sitting at his desk staring down into the street, started violently, guiltily, Gentry thought. His hand went out and picked up a letter lying on his desk. He dropped it into a drawer and closed the drawer.

Gentry said, "What's that?"

"Nothing. Nothing at all. What do you want, Harris?"

"I want to know what you just dropped in that drawer."

Kemmerer's face flushed with anger. His eyes blazed. "That," he said, "is none of your damn business. Now get out of here."

Gentry crossed the room to the judge's desk. He said, "Give me that letter, Judge. Or I'll take it from you."

Kemmerer's face now went white with fury. He got halfway to his feet before Gentry pushed him back. His hands began to shake and the anger faded from his eyes. Gentry repeated, "Give me the letter, Judge. Don't do anything you're going to be sorry for."

Kemmerer opened the drawer. He handed the letter to Gentry, who glanced at it, then ripped it open. He withdrew the letter, unfolded and read it swiftly. Deliberately, he tore it into tiny scraps and let them sift through his fingers to the floor.

Kemmerer stared up at him. His expression was a mixture of uncertainty, anger, fear and shame. He bent suddenly and yanked open the bottom right-hand drawer of his desk. His hand went into it and came back out clutching a small derringer.

Gentry swung the flat of his hand savagely. It struck the side of Kemmerer's face, rocked his head violently, and left an angry red mark. Gentry said, with clipped, military authority, "Drop it! Drop it or I'll jam it down your goddam throat!"

The derringer clattered to the floor. Gentry kicked it aside. He stared at Kemmerer, anger glittering coldly in his eyes. He said, "What the hell is the matter with you? Are you trying to ruin this whole damned town as well as yourself? You know what will happen if word of what happened to that man's brother gets out. You act like you were out of your mind!"

Kemmerer stared at the floor, refusing to look up and meet Gentry's eyes. He said, "You're going to kill him."

Gentry shook his head. "No. I'm not going to kill him. We are. Riker and Murphy and Brooks and Childers and myself. And you're going to be part of it because you know about it and will do nothing to stop it."

Kemmerer said, "It's dirty and it's evil. It's worse than what we did before. At least we did that in hot blood, in anger and outrage over what we thought the man had done. This is cold-blooded murder, what the law calls first-degree."

Gentry shrugged. "Maybe. But do you think murder is new to me? I sent men to certain death a dozen times during the war. I sent men to death trying to take a certain hill or house; and when they were all killed, then I sent in more to do the same thing the first bunch failed to do. If the second bunch failed, then I sent in a third. I have sent hundreds, thousands of men to their deaths—for nothing—for a lousy stone fence or a barn or a dirty, muddy depression in the ground. In most cases, their dying did not accomplish a single, God damned thing. This man's dying will save a town. Do you think, after all those useless deaths, I will shrink from a useful one?"

"But it's wrong! Can't you see that it's wrong? This isn't war."

"Isn't it? What is war, anyway? Two opposing forces struggling for supremacy, like Lane Sauer against the town. There are good men in this town, worthwhile men who will do worthwhile things. But not if Sauer spreads his story. Hell, Judge, even if we let him get away, if we let him spread his story, what earthly good would it do? Would it bring his brother back? Would it punish the men of Saguaro more than they have already punished themselves? No, it would only ruin them and their families."

The judge had nothing to say. Gentry, standing over him glaring, shouting, was overpowering. He made logic where there was no logic. He made wrong seem, for the moment, right. He would make a splendid career for himself in the years to come, Kemmerer thought. If the story of Jess Sauer's lynching remained a secret from the world.

Kemmerer watched him stride to the door. As Gentry pulled it open, he managed enough courage to say, "I will get another letter out. If I cannot do that, I will go out myself. This man's family is going to know what happened to him if I never do anything else."

Gentry froze for an instant. Then he said softly, "Judge, I hoped you wouldn't make me say this to you, but I have no choice. I will kill you myself if you write another

145

letter. I will kill you if you are instrumental in letting news of that lynching six months ago leak out. If you try to leave Saguaro, I will know what you mean to do and I will kill you. Is that clear?"

Kemmerer nodded silently, only wanting Gentry to leave, to close the door, to take himself from this office and from his presence.

For a long time after the door had closed, he stared at it. Then he got paper out of a drawer and began to write. Writing, he recognized a basic truth. If Gentry and the others meant to silence conscience in this town then the killing today would only be the first. They would have to kill again, and again, to keep news of the Sauer brothers' fate from the outside world. And even though they killed repeatedly, they would fail. They would fail for the simple reason that evil always fails.

Gentry was scowling blackly as he strode along the hall and down the stairs. He didn't know what had made Kemmerer so stubborn all of a sudden. Kemmerer had as much to lose as anyone. He had more to lose than most.

He stopped on the boardwalk a moment and glanced up at the bluff behind the town. No dust cloud lifted from the road at its crest. Gentry pulled his heavy gold watch from his pocket and looked at it. It was ten minutes of twelve. It was only a matter of minutes now. He had to get down to the jail before Manus saw the stage coming and started uptown.

But there was something else he had to do first. He crossed the street briskly, feeling sweat spring from his pores because of the exertion and the heat. He entered the post office. Batterton was behind the stage-line grille. Gentry said, "Ed, get over to the judge's office right away.

Don't let him write any letters and don't let him leave. Not until the stage is gone."

Batterton nodded, unconcealed relief in his eyes. Gentry realized that he was glad to get away from here where the shooting of Sauer was going to take place. He didn't want to witness it; he didn't want anything to do with it. Gentry said, "He's got a little derringer, so you'd better take a gun."

Batterton nodded, took a revolver from a shelf beneath the counter and stuck it into his belt. Becoming conscious of the weight of his own revolver in the side pocket of his coat, Gentry took it out, quickly checked the loads, then stuffed it into his belt.

Batterton hurried out, crossed the street and climbed the outside stairs. He disappeared into the door at their head.

Gentry went out. Again he glanced at the top of the bluff, then turned and walked past the hotel toward the jail. He saw Nicolo Finch sitting on the hotel veranda watching him. He saw Lane Sauer sitting inside the lobby close to one of the large windows.

He was glad this part of the job was his. He would not have wanted to be the one who actually had to kill the man. Yet it suited his prominence and importance in the community to have an essential part in the undertaking. Holding the sheriff at the jail, preventing him from interfering, was such an essential part.

In Gentry's mind, Lane Sauer was already dead.

CHAPTER 17

Nicolo Finch watched Gentry come from the office building across the street. He saw him go into the post office
and a few moments later saw Ed Batterton come out,
cross the street and climb the stairs Gentry had just come
down.

He frowned. He was aware of the tension in the street
this morning, even though his mind could not pinpoint
precisely what it was coming from. It was just a feeling,
he supposed, an instinct for danger more strongly devel-
oped in men who live with nature and with solitude.

Gentry came from the post office, stood for a moment,
then glanced up at the top of the ridge. As plainly as
words, the gesture said he was waiting for the stage. He
turned then, and walked past the hotel. He angled across
the street, either toward Newkirk's saloon or the jail,
farther on.

Finch frowned to himself. Something had bothered him
about Gentry this morning . . . something was different
. . . but for the life of him, he couldn't decide what it
was.

His body tense, his eyes worried, he watched the man.
Gentry walked like an army officer, he thought. There was
an air of assurance to him, an aura of command. . . .

Gentry went past Newkirk's, without stopping. He went on toward the jail. It had to be the jail, Finch thought.

Gentry turned in at the jail and disappeared.

Finch frowned again. Something kept bothering him. It was normal enough for Gentry to go to the sheriff's office, he supposed. Gentry was a lawyer and often had business with Manus down at the jail.

Yet he knew something was out of the ordinary today. And suddenly he realized what it was. Gentry had been carrying a gun. Stuffed in his belt in front, there had been a gun.

Finch had never seen Gentry carry one before, so its presence now was incongruous. There had to be a reason for it on this particular morning and Finch immediately thought he knew what the reason was. Gentry intended to keep the sheriff off the street, out of the violence planned for Lane Sauer when the stage came in.

He got to his feet. He glanced up at the ridge and saw a cloud of dust raise in the clear, hot, desert air. He stepped off the veranda, wincing slightly and unconsciously as the sun struck him with its appalling, searing heat.

The stage would be rolling down River Street in another five minutes. That was about the time it took for the coach to negotiate the steep road off the ridge.

Not much time, he thought. But enough, if nothing slowed him down, if he didn't run into too much trouble at the jail. He hurried that way, feeling the sweat drench him immediately. His hand dropped and unconsciously touched the walnut grips of his holstered gun.

Down at the lower end of the street, Otto Riker came to the wide double doors of the livery barn. He untied his leather blacksmith's apron and hung it on a nail beside

149

Baldwinsville Library

the door. He stared up River Street, lifting his glance to the top of the bluff beyond. He saw the dust cloud raise, a moment later saw the six horses and the coach appear out of the dust. Faintly he heard the driver's shout.

The stage began its descent. Riker wiped his hands on the legs of his pants and started up the street.

There was no shade at this time of day. The sun was directly overhead. Riker squinted against the glare. He saw a man step off the hotel veranda and come toward him, but it was not the stranger. It looked to Riker like Nicolo Finch.

What the hell was Finch doing in town today, he wondered. He'd been in town only yesterday and had hired a horse immediately after the stage came in to ride on out to the ranch.

Finch angled across the street and headed toward the jail. Riker's frown deepened.

He held his pace to a slow walk, trying to time himself so that the stage would arrive before he did. It was almost halfway down the ridge road now.

Narrowing his eyes, he stared at the hotel veranda. He didn't see Lane Sauer yet. He was probably still in the hotel. He glanced at Murphy's gunsmith shop but he couldn't see anything there either. He was still too far away.

Tension began to grow in him. He didn't think he would get a chance to mix it up with Sauer, but he was still hoping that he would. He wanted another chance at Sauer. He wanted to prove to himself, the town, and to Sauer that he could break the stranger in two.

He passed the jail. Glancing in, he saw Gentry talking to Manus. Gentry's back was to him, Manus facing him. The sheriff's face was flushed and he looked angry.

Riker went past. He saw Mrs. Gentry approaching now from the direction of Childers' mercantile.

Sauer came through the lobby door and stepped out onto the hotel veranda, a valise in his left hand.

Riker slowed involuntarily with a glance at the stage dusting rapidly down the twisting road. He felt hatred burning inside him suddenly. He felt his powerful hands clench, relax and clench again.

The intensity of this hatred made him frown unexpectedly with puzzlement. Why did he hate Sauer so? Because of the fight last night in which he had not come out quite as well as he should? He shook his head slowly. The fight last night had nothing to do with it. Neither did the threat of exposure if Sauer got away.

No. It went back to the night of the lynching six months before. His hatred was not really for this man at all but for his brother, who was dead but who had spit in his face just before he died.

The whole town had seen that. The whole town had seen Sauer express his contempt of Riker by spitting squarely into his face.

Anger and reflex had brought Riker's quirt slashing down instantly against the horse's rump. The horse had plunged away, jerking Sauer from the saddle, breaking his neck, leaving him twisting grotesquely at the end of the rope.

The town had turned its face away. In Riker's flash of sudden rage, the men of the town had caught their first glimpse of the evil in what they had just done. And seeing it, they had turned their faces away, leaving Riker alone, the quirt in his hand, the whole terrible responsibility for Sauer's death resting squarely on him.

He remembered standing there, the dead man's spittle still on his face, the quirt dangling from his trembling hand. He remembered wiping his face with a sleeve. But most of all he remembered the way not a single one of them would look at him. They'd found a whipping boy.

They'd found a goat. Each of them could henceforth tell himself that Riker was the one who had killed Sauer. Without Riker it would not have been possible because no one else in town would have used the whip.

That wasn't true, of course. Newkirk would have taken Riker's place. Or his place would have been taken by someone else. The town had wanted to kill that night, and would have killed, with or without Riker, or Newkirk, or any other single individual.

He stared angrily up the street. He glowered at Nicolo Finch as he passed the man, but he did not speak. Finch was one of them. Gentry was another. They were all involved and now he was getting ready to fish their chestnuts out of the fire a second time. But he was damned if he knew why.

What did he want from the people of this town that he didn't already have? He wanted respect, he realized suddenly. He wanted somebody to call him Mister Riker for a change.

That was why he'd served as executioner that night. It was why he was walking up River Street right now, prepared to remove another threat to Saguaro's citizens.

But he had a sudden, dismal certainty that he was going about it wrong. He wasn't earning their respect but only their contempt. He was doing something they wouldn't dirty their own hands doing and that was no way to get respect from them.

But it was the only thing he knew that he could do.

The bottle in front of Jake Newkirk was half empty when he saw Gentry pass on his way to the jail farther down the street. A few moments later, Finch went past, heading the same way. Almost immediately thereafter, Riker came into sight, going the other way. Belle Gentry passed Riker in front of the saloon. The stage must be coming in, he thought.

He circled the bar and headed for the door. Reaching it, he yelled, "Riker!"

Riker swung his head and scowled. He stopped, but he did not approach closer than he was. He glanced from Newkirk toward the hotel and then back to Newkirk again. He asked, "What do *you* want?"

Newkirk went through the swinging doors and stepped into the blinding sun. Suddenly furious at Riker's tone, he said, "I hope he blows your head off!"

Riker scowled. "What the hell's the matter with you? You been eatin' raw meat or something?"

Jake turned his head. Gentry had disappeared. Finch was almost to the jail, with Belle Gentry close behind. He stared at Riker again. "You lousy killer!"

Riker's face suddenly looked murderous. "You son of a bitch, what are you so damned righteous about? Your hands ain't exactly clean. You led that mob. Without you, there wouldn't have been no mob."

"You're the one that whipped his horse out from under him." The sun made Jake's head reel. He felt dizzy and almost sick.

"Yeah, and I wish I hadn't too. For a woman like her! For a bitch that ought to have been down there in the cribs instead of uptown with all the big men callin' on her!"

Jake wished he hadn't had so much to drink. He wished he could see Riker more clearly. He wanted to rush him, to beat him down into the dirt and choke him with his hands. But he knew he'd fall down before he got to Riker. And even if he didn't, Riker would knock him down with a single blow.

What he needed was a gun. He'd kill Riker, by God, that's what he'd do. He'd show him. He'd show everyone.

Maybe he wouldn't stop with Riker. Maybe he'd kill Childers while he was at it. And Brooks. And Gentry too.

He muttered, "You lousy killer! You lousy killer!"

Riker glared furiously at him. He took a step toward him, then stopped and glanced up the street toward the ridge. The stage was nearly to the bottom of the grade. Another switchback and one more curve and it would be entering River Street.

Riker growled, "I'll get to you later, Jake. You want a fight, you'll get a fight."

He stalked away.

Jake stared at him helplessly a moment. He wished he had a gun right now. If he did, he'd blow a hole in that damned Riker's skull. . . . He bawled, "You lousy killer! You damn lousy killer!"

Riker didn't turn his head but his neck got red. Jake wheeled and staggered back through the swinging doors into his saloon. He was drunk now. He knew he was drunk, but he didn't care. He was going to get even with a lot of people today. He was going to clean a lot of slates.

He staggered across the room toward the bar. He fell against a table and it overturned. He went down in a heap.

He pulled himself upright again. Slowly, with exaggerated care, he walked to the bar and along it until he reached its end. He rounded it and reached under the counter.

There were two guns here, a double-barreled shotgun and a rifle. Both were loaded. Jake laid them on top of the bar and stared drunkenly at them. The shotgun held but two cartridges, he realized, but the rifle held six. He put the shotgun back beneath the bar.

Picking up the rifle, he levered a cartridge into the chamber. He eased the hammer down to half cock. He threw the rifle to his shoulder and sighted at the door.

154

The sights were blurred and so was the door. He shook his head almost angrily but his vision did not clear.

He shouldn't have had so much to drink, but maybe if he went out back and doused his head . . .

Unsteadily he went out the back door, leaving the rifle on the bar. He worked the pump hurriedly until it gushed a stream of clear, cold water. He stuck his head under it.

In this heat, the coldness of the water was a shock. He straightened, shaking his head. He ran his fingers through his hair and went back inside.

He picked up the rifle again and sighted at the door. Things weren't fuzzy any more.

He started toward the door, then stopped reluctantly, thinking of Riker, thinking what the blacksmith would do to him if he missed. He'd wait just a little while, he decided. He'd wait until his head cleared just a little more. He didn't want to make any mistakes today. He wanted all of them, Riker and the other three.

He heard the stagecoach rattling down River Street, heard the pound of hoofs on the hard-packed ground. He heard the driver shout. . . .

He walked to the door with deliberate care. He stopped and waited there, watching the movement of people in the street, holding the loaded rifle tightly in his shaking hands.

CHAPTER 18

When Saralee saw the dust cloud at the top of the ridge, she got instantly to her feet. She picked up the valise she had packed for herself and said, "It's coming. Pick up your bag and come on. Or stay here. I can't make you go, but I'm going whether you do or not."

She opened the door. Severo stared at her numbly, without moving or speaking. She stepped out onto the gallery and closed the door. She turned and hurried along the packed earth walk to the street.

The door opened behind her. Glancing around, she saw her father come from the house, carrying the small carpet-bag she had packed for him. He called, "Wait. . . ."

She halted, smiling at him. He was scowling angrily, and when he reached her, he growled, "Of all the damn fool things . . . I must be crazy to listen to you."

She walked along the street toward the hotel. Her father kept pace, scowling but not talking any more. In seconds, his face was dripping with sweat. He pushed back his hat and wiped his forehead with his hand.

They reached River Street. The coach was negotiating the last turn before entering River Street at its upper end.

She saw Riker angling across toward the hotel. She saw

Finch, almost to the jail. Mrs. Gentry was running after him, skirts lifted so that she would not trip on them.

Saralee hurried across the street, with Severo only a step behind. Reaching the hotel, she saw Lane Sauer looking out one of the lobby windows at her.

She turned her head and glanced at Riker, lounging now in front of the post office. He was unarmed. Glancing across the street, she saw Murphy standing in the door of his shop.

Suddenly she began to shiver violently, as though from cold. She wanted to run, to scream, to get away from the overpowering feeling of menace here on this familiar main street of the town she knew so well. But she didn't move, except to put her bag down on the walk. She waited, her head turned to watch the stagecoach careening down the street, followed by a towering cloud of dust.

Behind Saralee, Meyer opened the lobby door and stepped out onto the veranda, his bag in his hand. Quickly, almost furtively, he sidled along the veranda until he reached its end. Here he sank into a chair, removed his hat and wiped his streaming forehead with his handkerchief. His bag rested between his feet.

The street looked commonplace. Riker was the only one visible, except for a woman hurrying toward the jail, except for the gunsmith standing in the open door of his shop across the street, and except for the waitress from the hotel dining room and her drunken father, who were also apparently waiting for the stage.

Meyer glanced at her and quickly glanced away, not wanting her to catch his glance, wanting no sign of recognition to betray the fact that she had spoken to him earlier today about getting Sauer's letter out. She must have decided to try leaving town, he thought, and, knowing what the town's secret was, wondered if they would let her leave.

His uneasiness steadily increased. Instead of stopping Sauer and the girl right here in town, what if they pursued the stage and attacked it on the road? He stared down at his trembling hands. To hell with it. If Sauer and that girl got on the stage, then he was going to stay behind. He could always wait until tomorrow.

Belle Gentry lifted her skirts and ran. Her husband was no longer in sight, having disappeared into the sheriff's office. The cowboy from the ranch east of town was now only a dozen yards ahead of her. His destination seemed to be the same as hers. He also seemed to be headed toward the jail.

Finch did not look around. When he was but fifty feet from the jail, he drew his gun and thereafter held it in his hand.

Terror gave Belle extra speed. She was out of breath but she did not slow her frantic pace. She had seen the gun stuffed into her husband's belt. She knew he intended to use it, against the sheriff or against the brother of the man they'd lynched six months ago. She also knew she had to stop him if she could. She had to stop him from becoming a murderer again.

Ahead of her, Finch reached the jail and stopped before the door. Belle ran up behind him and stopped. She saw Manus facing the door, his hands up, held at shoulder height. She saw her husband's back, and the gun in his hand. She saw him whirl as Finch said harshly, "Drop it, Gentry. Drop that gun!"

Everything was confusion after that. Harris whirling, the gun in his hand flashing, belching out a cloud of black powder smoke. Something struck her a numbing blow.

She felt herself falling, felt the shock of the boardwalk

as she struck it. Then she was staring up at the blazing sun and her head was whirling, spinning, turning around and around . . .

She heard Finch's voice, "Damn you, drop that gun or I'll blow your head off!" She heard what sounded like the clatter of a gun on the wooden floor. And she heard Burt Manus say, "All right, Gentry, back into one of those cells. Move, damn you, before I bend this gun over your head!"

The iron cell door slammed thunderously. She saw Manus' face above her, and that of the cowboy Finch. Manus said anxiously, "Get Saralee, Finch. Hurry up. I think she's hurt pretty bad."

Back in his cell, Gentry began to yell. "Manus! Burt! Let me out of here. Belle's hurt. Damn you, Manus, let me out of here!"

Manus growled, "Shut up, Gentry. Shut up. Finch is going after Saralee." He knelt beside Belle. "Can you hear me, Mrs. Gentry?"

She tried to nod her head. The sheriff said, "I'm going to pick you up and carry you inside. It'll probably hurt but I'll be as careful as I can."

She closed her eyes. She felt him slip his hands beneath her and felt herself lifted. For a brief instant the pain was terrible. She heard a scream. The sound seemed to be coming from someone else yet she knew that was impossible.

Almost immediately, her husband began yelling again. Manus laid her down carefully on the office couch. He straightened and said harshly, "Shut up, Gentry."

"Burt! For God's sake, let me go to her. I did it. I shot her, but I swear to God it was an accident!"

"Sure it was an accident. You meant to shoot Nicolo Finch."

159

"I didn't mean to shoot anyone. I only wanted to keep you here until after the stage got in."

"Why?"

Gentry didn't answer him. There was a moment's silence, then Gentry pleaded, "Burt, please! You can't keep me in here when Belle may be dying out there. I won't run away. You know I won't run away."

"Damn right you won't. You'll stay right there until you tell me what's going to happen when the stage comes in."

"Burt, for Christ's sake . . ."

Manus didn't bother to answer him.

Half a minute ticked away. At last Gentry yelled, "All right! I'll tell you. Riker's going to jump Sauer. If Sauer goes for his gun, Murphy's going to blast him from across the street!"

"That's all?"

"Yes, that's all! I swear that's all! Now let me out! Let me look after Belle!"

So unmistakable was the anguish in his voice that a light smile touched Belle Gentry's grayish lips. She felt suddenly warm where previously she had been cold. She heard the key turn in the lock, heard the iron door swing back. She heard footsteps, then felt her husband's presence at her side. She felt the warmth of his breath, felt his tears drop into her face. He said brokenly, "Belle, I didn't mean to do it. I wouldn't hurt you. You know I wouldn't hurt you, don't you, Belle?"

She licked her lips and tried to speak, but she didn't have the strength. She groped for his hand, found it and held on tight. She could hold him here. She could keep him at her side until whatever was going to happen in front of the hotel was over with. Harris would have no part in Lane Sauer's death.

Her head began to whirl. The room reeled crazily before

her eyes. She felt as though she were falling, down, down. . . .

All the world turned black. But her hand, holding that of her husband, did not relax.

Saralee heard the revolver shot from the direction of the jail. She yanked her head that way automatically in time to see Belle Gentry slump to the boardwalk, where she lay completely still.

She turned her head and looked at the approaching coach. She shifted her glance to her father's face.

Manus came out of the jail. He spoke to Finch, who came hurrying toward her. The sheriff knelt, picked Belle up and carried her inside.

Saralee watched Finch run diagonally across the street. He was coming for her. She was the one they always sent for when someone had been hurt.

She turned her head toward the window where she had last seen Lane. He was no longer visible.

Something almost like panic stirred in her. She would be gone when the trouble erupted here. She wouldn't be able to help him in any way. She'd be down at the jail helping Belle Gentry until long after the stage had gone. . . .

Rebellion touched her briefly. She'd refuse, she thought. Let someone else help Belle. They had no right to ask this of her, no right to keep her here in Saguaro when she wanted to leave on the stage today.

Finch was close now, less than fifty yards away. He called, "Miss Vargas! The sheriff wants you down at the jail. Mrs. Gentry has been shot!"

Once more Saralee stared at her father. His face was a study of conflicting emotions. He was relieved because this meant they would not be leaving on the stage, but he was disappointed too because he had worked up his courage for nothing if they did not leave today.

She said, "Wait here, Father. Send someone for me just before the stage is due to leave."

He nodded wordlessly. She saw Lane Sauer come out of the lobby door and stand on the veranda, his eyes squinting against the glare. His face was puffy and bruised from his encounter with Riker last night. But he was wearing his gun and the way it hung told her he was no novice in the use of it.

Finch reached her. He started to repeat what he had called out to her moments before, but she stopped him with her words, "I'm coming. I'm coming right away."

Perhaps Finch saw the anguish in her face. Perhaps he saw the way she looked at Lane. He said softly, urgently, "The sheriff is coming, ma'am. He knows what Riker's got in mind."

She nodded. Every instant she stood here reduced Belle Gentry's chances to live. Suddenly she turned and ran toward the jail.

She could hear the pound of the coach horses' hoofs in the dusty street as she ran. She could hear the squeak of thorough braces and the rattle of tugs and trees. She could hear the crack of the driver's whip and his high, thin yell.

She thought fleetingly and ironically that these little touches, the noisy, hurried arrival of the daily stage, the driver's shouts, the plunging, sweating horses, the swaying rattling coach . . . all these things gave the coach's arrival new drama and excitement every day. Except that today there was no need for it. Today there was enough drama in the baking, dusty street. Death stalked the street today, only waiting for the arrival of the stage.

Almost to the jail, she turned her head and looked back. Finch was standing on the hotel veranda fifteen or twenty feet from Lane. Lane still waited immediately before the door. Meyer sat in a chair at the farthest corner of the veranda. The coach was less than a block away and coming fast. Riker began to walk toward Severo, ignoring Lane Sauer as though he wasn't even there.

Saralee went through the open door into the jail. Belle Gentry was lying on the leather-covered office couch. Her husband knelt on the floor beside her, holding onto her hand. Burt Manus waited beside the door, a double-barreled shotgun in his hands. As soon as Saralee came in, he went out, disappearing from her sight.

It took every bit of will Saralee could muster to cross the room, to turn her back on what was about to happen in the street. Her face was pale, her lips compressed.

Harris Gentry looked up at her. "Is she dead? Is she . . . ?"

Saralee put her hand on Belle's wrist. The pulse was weak but regular. She stared at the blood on the front of Belle Gentry's dress. She said sharply, "Go away. Go to the window and turn your back to us."

Gentry hesitated. Then he released his hand from that of his wife and got awkwardly to his feet. He looked down at her, turned and crossed to the window.

Saralee said, "I want you to tell me everything that happens in the street. If you leave, I will leave too. Is that clear?"

"Yes'm." Gentry's voice was no longer that of a Confederate colonel of cavalry.

Saralee began to rip Belle Gentry's dress away to uncover the ugly wound. She knew it was hopeless. Belle Gentry was going to die.

But until she did, Saralee had to stay with her. She had to do all she could. She owed that to Belle and she owed it to herself.

CHAPTER 19

Ed Batterton was out of breath by the time he reached the top of the stairs. He paused for an instant on the landing and stared back down into the street. The hotel seemed to drowse in the sun. The post office next door looked equally sleepy.

Both appearances were deceptive. In a few minutes all hell was going to break loose down there. Thank God he was here. Thank God he wouldn't be involved.

His hand, bony and blue-veined, touched the grip of the revolver he had stuffed into his belt. He opened the door and stepped into the hallway leading to Gentry's office and that of the judge. Hearing a faint shout, he turned his head and glanced up at the ridge. The stage was coming, raising a towering cloud of dust as it lurched down the steep road behind the town.

He closed the door behind him and stared along the hall. He withdrew the gun from his belt and thumbed the hammer back. Gentry had told him to hold the judge up here until everything was over in the street. Gentry thought the judge might intervene.

Batterton walked silently along the hall to the judge's door. He stopped here, his hand trembling, his stomach cramping suddenly as though he was about to be sick.

How he had ever managed to get himself involved in this, he didn't know. That night six months ago now seemed like a bad dream, a nightmare, something that hadn't happened at all. Yet he knew it had happened. He knew how real it was. It was so real that the man across the street in the hotel was about to be killed just for being here, just for knowing what had happened to his brother six months earlier.

He opened the door suddenly. Judge Kemmerer was sitting in his swivel chair, turned so that he could look into the street. He whirled the chair as Batterton came in and stared surprisedly at the gun in the postmaster's hand.

Batterton's voice sounded abnormally shrill as he said, "Don't make any sudden moves, Judge. Just sit right where you are."

Kemmerer continued to stare at him. Batterton found his steady glance unnerving. He looked past the judge and out of the window into the street. Kemmerer asked, "Gentry send you here?"

"Never mind who sent me. Just sit tight until the stage leaves town."

"Do you know what they're going to do?"

Batterton nodded.

Kemmerer was looking strangely at him. He asked, "Do you realize that you'll be just as guilty of his death as the man who pulls the trigger?"

"You'd have a hell of a time proving that."

Kemmerer nodded. "Yes, I suppose I would. But you'll know it, won't you, Ed? You'll know it until the day you die."

"Sit still, Judge, and shut up. We've all gone too far to back out now."

Kemmerer nodded sadly, reluctantly. "Yes. I suppose we have." He stared at the gun in Ed Batterton's trembling hand.

Across the street from the hotel, Frank Murphy watched as the stage negotiated the last turn and entered River Street at its upper end.

He could see Riker waiting across the street. He could see the others—Finch, Meyers, Severo Vargas—and the stranger, Sauer, who had just come out of the hotel.

He backed away from the door, the rifle in his hand. He reached the counter, which ran the width of the store, went around behind it, knelt and rested the rifle on the counter top.

He sighted carefully on Sauer's chest. He moved the sights from dead center to a place slightly to the left where he knew the man's heart was. He waited, hands trembling slightly but not enough to spoil his aim.

There was a strange excitement in him now. He had heard the shot down at the jail a few moments before, but had not bothered to look out of the door. He had seen Finch come after Saralee and had seen her run that way. Someone had been shot down there but it didn't affect him or what he and Riker were going to do. Riker was still waiting over across the street. The stranger was also there.

He shifted the sights until they rested on Riker's chest. He smiled faintly to himself. A gun gave a man a feeling of power nothing else ever could. Right now he held Riker's life in the palm of his hand. He was as big as Riker was, and as powerful. Hell, with this rifle in his hands he was a sight bigger than Riker could ever be.

He shifted the sights back to Sauer's chest. A light frown touched his broad, normally smooth brow.

166

He was thinking of Lorina now. Thinking of her and remembering how he had wanted her, how she had laughed at him. Mainly, he supposed, because he was three inches shorter than she.

He'd been glad when he heard that she was dead. He'd been glad when he found out why it had been done—because she had refused her killer. Because, after making him want her, she had refused him and taunted him. The way she once had taunted Frank.

A lot of people in town had thought Lorina was an angel, but she was a long, long ways from that. She had been a devil and he was glad she was dead.

He didn't exactly know why he'd gone along with the mob that night. He didn't hate Lorina's killer like the others did. He guessed he had gone along because he didn't want to be singled out as different.

Different. His face twisted slightly and his eyes narrowed until they were only slits. He *was* different. He was short and squat and thick. Everything about him was thick and coarse. His head was too big for the rest of his body. Even the crib girls tried to get out of going with him. But he was like other men inside. He had the same wants and desires as other men.

Staring at Lane Sauer now over the muzzle of his gun, he knew why he'd helped hang Sauer's brother that night six months ago. He also knew why he'd helped Riker beat Sauer last night in the saloon, and why he'd agreed to stand here with a rifle in his hands today. Because Sauer was tall and slender and straight—because he was all the things Murphy wanted to be but never could be. Sauer was the kind, he thought bitterly, who could have any woman he wanted. Sauer's brother had been that kind too. Murphy had seen the way Lorina looked at him that night in the hotel dining room.

He could hear the stage coming now, could hear the driver's shouts, the hard pound of hoofs on the hard-packed, dusty street, the rattle of tugs and doubletrees.

He held his careful bead on Lane Sauer's chest, knowing he was out of sight back here in the dimness of his store.

Childers heard the shot at the jail and instantly stepped out of the front door of his store. He saw Manus come out of the jail, saw him lift the inert body of a woman from the boardwalk and carry her inside. The woman looked like Belle.

He scowled angrily. Gentry had gone down there to keep the sheriff there. He wondered suddenly what had happened to him.

He shifted his glance across the street to the group in front of the hotel. Nicolo Finch came running from the jail, calling for Saralee. After several moments she ran toward the jail.

He stared at Riker, in front of the post office. The stage was coming now; it was almost here.

Riker would do his job. Murphy would do his. Everything would come off fine provided Manus didn't intervene. But he couldn't be sure of that any more. Manus had come out of the jail and picked Belle Gentry up. He'd carried her inside. His doing so was evidence that Gentry must be either dead, knocked out or locked up in a cell. Otherwise he'd have come out after Belle himself.

Childers backed into his store. Hurrying now, he went to the rear of it and got the shotgun he kept there. It was always loaded, but he checked now to make sure it was.

He'd be conspicuous, coming into the street armed, particularly since he was armed with a shotgun instead of with something he could conceal. But it couldn't be helped. A shotgun was the only thing that would put the fear of God in Burt. A revolver wouldn't scare him at all.

The stage was less than a hundred yards away as Childers stepped out of his store again. The driver's face was white as it turned toward Childers in surprise.

Childers raised a hand, grinned and waved at the driver to reassure him. He stopped, waiting for the stage to pass in front of him.

As the stage went past, the driver pulled in his teams. Plunging, they slowed, drawing toward the opposite side of the street as they did.

The cloud of dust raised by their hoofs and by the iron-tired wheels was blinding, choking. Childers began to cough.

For a moment everything was obscured by dust, which drifted across toward Childers' side of the street. He turned his head and glanced toward the jail. He didn't see anyone down there but he did see Harry Zeeb stick his head out the door of his furniture store. Zeeb's face was white and scared. He withdrew almost immediately.

Childers stood there, legs spread, the shotgun in his hands, staring toward the jail. He was thinking that of all the men in town, only a few were willing to do what had to be done today. Gentry. Himself. Riker and Murphy. The others were either too terrified or they had suddenly acquired scruples they hadn't had six months ago.

The dust was settling. Riker, who had been in front of the post office when the stage came in, was now walking toward the hotel. The stage horses, excited by the descent of the hill and the wild gallop into town, were plunging and fidgeting.

Childers stared at Riker's face. The man's eyes were narrowed and glittering. There was a set to his mouth that was ugly. His shoulders were hunched forward and for an instant he reminded Childers of a bull pawing the ground before a charge.

He saw Lane Sauer step from the hotel veranda, his bag in his hand. Sauer started toward the coach.

Childers glanced along the street toward Murphy's shop. If Riker didn't hurry, Sauer would get behind the coach. Murphy wouldn't be able to shoot at him.

Riker began to run. He passed from Childers' sight behind the coach.

Dust was still settling in the street. Childers walked to the outside stairway that ascended to the office over the furniture store. He stood there, waiting, the shotgun held negligently in his hands.

In a few more minutes it would be over, he thought. Sauer would be dead. Manus would be helpless, even to make an arrest, because it would be obvious Sauer had been killed while drawing his gun against an unarmed man.

But those few minutes would be the longest in Childers' experience. They would drag on and on for what seemed an eternity.

CHAPTER 20

The coach was pulling to a halt in front of the stage-line office up the street as the sheriff left his office. Manus saw Holt Childers in front of the furniture store, a shotgun in his hands. He saw Lane Sauer step down off the veranda and head for the coach. He did not see Riker at all and assumed he was hidden behind the coach.

He strode along purposefully, cutting diagonally across the street. He saw Riker come from behind the stage and head toward Lane.

He began to run. Damn! He was going to be too late. Not much. A couple of seconds at most. But enough. Lane Sauer was going to be killed in spite of everything he could do. The range of the shotgun he carried was too short. He needed a rifle but it was too late now to go back for one.

In his office over the furniture store, Kemmerer stared at the postmaster, and at the gun in Batterton's hand. A letter was before him on the desk, a letter to which he had just affixed his signature. He opened a desk drawer and reached for an envelope. Batterton stiffened and Kemmerer said, "I'm just getting an envelope."

He withdrew the envelope and wrote the name of

Sauer's father and his address on it. He put the letter inside, lighted a candle and dripped sealing wax on the flap. He pushed a seal into the wax.

Batterton asked, "Who's that going to?"

Kemmerer glanced up at him. "It's going to Sauer's family. I'm going to put it on the stage myself. If you're planning to stop me, you'd better screw up your courage, because you're going to have to shoot me." He studied Batterton briefly, then got to his feet. He could see the derringer lying on the floor behind the desk where Gentry had kicked it earlier. He paid no attention to it. He didn't intend to fight with Batterton. The postmaster would have to shoot him or let him go. He wasn't going to make the choice easy by trying to reach the derringer.

He looked Batterton squarely in the eye. He said, "Ed, I've known you for a long, long time, haven't I?"

"What's that got to do with it?"

Kemmerer shrugged. "Nothing maybe. Only I think I know you as well as I know anyone. I don't think you can shoot a man in cold blood." He paused a moment, then went on. "I'm going out of here. I'm going down the stairs and across the street. I'm going to give this letter to the stage driver. If you're going to stop me, now's the time for it."

Deliberately, he turned his back. He walked slowly to the door. He stopped with his hand on the knob, waiting. Then he opened the door and stepped through.

He heard no sound behind him except for Batterton's harsh breathing. He fought a compulsion to look around, knowing if he did he would make it that much easier for Batterton to shoot.

He walked along the hall, wanting to run, but forcing himself to maintain a slow and steady walk.

Outside in the street he could hear the pound of the

coach horses' hoofs, the yelling of the driver, the rattle of harness rings and tugs. He opened the door leading to the stairs.

Suddenly, he turned his head, unable to resist the compulsion any more. Batterton was standing in his office doorway, gun leveled, eye squinting along the barrel. He was going to fire. Good God, he was going to shoot!

Kemmerer tried to duck aside, knowing even as he did that he would be too late. He saw the flash, saw the puff of black powder smoke and felt something like a horse's kick in his thigh.

He was driven through the doorway and across the landing. He crashed against the wooden rail, smashed it and toppled for an instant at the edge of the landing fifteen feet above the ground.

Then he fell, soundlessly, helplessly, his arms and legs thrown out as though to slow his passage through the air.

He landed flat on his back. The air gusted violently out of his lungs. He lay there, bleeding, unable to move, sure this was the end and that he was going to die.

The letter, which had slipped out of his hand at the top of the stairs, fluttered through the air and landed at Holt Childers' feet. He stooped and picked it up. He glanced at it, then slipped it into his pocket.

Batterton appeared at the head of the stairs, the smoking gun still clutched in his hand. He came to the edge of the landing and stared down at the unmoving, bloody body of the judge. He raised his hands to cover his face, shocked by the realization of what he had done.

He seemed suddenly to become aware of the gun. He held it away and stared at it. Dazedly he turned his head and stared down at the stagecoach, just now stopping across the street.

He stepped back into the doorway. He raised the gun

and put the muzzle against his head. He thumbed back the hammer and pulled the trigger.

Childers glanced up when he heard the shot but he couldn't see anything. Batterton lay half in and half out of the door, hidden from his eyes. There was a growing pool of blood beneath his shattered skull.

As the stagecoach whirled to a stop, Lane Sauer heard, over the racket that it made, the sound of the shot that blew out Batterton's brains. The sound of the other one had been drowned by the racket of the arriving stage. At the same time he heard Riker bawl, "Sauer! You sonofabitch, I told you to get out of town!"

He'd been watching Riker and thought he knew why the man was there. Now he turned his glance full on the man.

Riker was unarmed and meant to kill him with his hands, he thought, right here in the street in front of everyone. He frowned worriedly, knowing that was far too simple a plan to be believed. There had to be more to it than that.

He glanced up at the stairway across the street and saw the body lying half in, half outside the door.

Childers stood at the bottom of the stairs. Beyond him, lying flat, was another body, one Lane didn't recognize. He turned his head and watched Riker approach. He could not control the bitter smile that touched his mouth. Already three of the townspeople were either wounded or dead.

They might kill him before they let him go on the stage. They might stop him from leaving town and telling the story of Saguaro's shame. But they were paying too.

Riker was close now, less than twenty feet away. Lane called sharply, "Hold it, Riker! I'm not going to mix it up with you again today. Hold it right where you are or I'll use my gun."

Staring at the hulking blacksmith, at his incredibly powerful arms and hands, Lane began to hurt again, in his ribs, in his chest, in his belly. His words didn't slow Riker. The blacksmith kept coming at the same steady rate, but there was a change in his expression. Lane's hand started toward his gun even as he puzzled over it. Riker's expression was triumphant. That was it. Lane's threat to use his gun had brought a look of triumph to Riker's ugly face.

And suddenly he understood. Even as his hand streaked toward the grip of his gun, he understood. Riker was unarmed. He knew Lane wouldn't take another beating at his hands. He knew Lane would go for his gun before he did.

Someone was waiting—somewhere—with his sights on Lane's chest right now. . . .

His hand touched his gun. At the same instant he flung himself forward desperately.

He felt the twitch of his shirt as the bullet tugged at it. He heard the report, loud, sharply vicious in the heat-baked street. The sound was that of a rifle, big-bored, carrying a big charge of powder. Maybe a buffalo gun. It boomed across the street, freezing each of the people there but making the coach horses begin to plunge and rear.

Lane's gun was in his hand and out. He continued his plunge toward Riker, not yet knowing where the bullet had come from so unexpectedly. Riker had stopped and was staring around puzzledly. The triumph was gone from his eyes. He seemed confused, as though he didn't quite know what to do in the face of this unforeseen development. Lane, the victim, should have been dead but he wasn't dead. He was very much alive.

175

From the hotel veranda, a handgun roared, once, twice. Finch held his revolver at eye level, sighting at something diagonally across the street.

Riker turned suddenly and plunged away from Lane. Lane swung his head briefly to stare across the street.

Murphy stood in the door of his shop, a heavy rifle in his hands. He was leaning against the doorjamb and he wasn't looking at Lane. He wasn't looking at anything. His eyes were blank.

Even as Lane watched, he began to buckle, to slide down the doorjamb to the floor. His feet jammed against the jamb on the other side and the rifle went out in front of him, propping his upper body so that it could not collapse.

But the man was dead. His head lolled forward until all Lane could see was the top of it. Lane's mind counted "Four." Four were now hurt or dead in the town of Saguaro. Four had paid the price for the lynching six months before.

The stagecoach driver was trying to quiet his teams. He sat on the box, reins in his hands, yelling curses at the frightened horses. Riker swung his head and his glance touched the driver's shotgun beside him on the seat. He lunged toward the coach.

Lane had a choice. He could shoot Riker before he reached the gun. If he did he would be wide open for a murder charge. He couldn't prove Riker was going for the driver's scattergun.

Or he could wait. He could hold off until Riker had the gun in his hands and then shoot him down, knowing if he did wait Riker might very well get off a shot before he fell. And at this range he couldn't miss.

Lane knew he had to wait. He had no other choice.

If he shot Riker before the man got his hands on that shotgun, he'd hang. Just like his brother had.

Riker reached the coach. He put a foot on the wheel hub and pulled himself high enough to seize the gun. Having done so, he pushed himself away and dropped to the ground. The driver bawled, "Hey, gimme back my gun!"

Lane fired as the gaping shotgun muzzle swung toward him. He was already in motion, knowing if he didn't find some cover Riker was going to cut him in two. His bullet missed cleanly because of the unexpected impetus Riker had given himself by pushing backward as he dropped from the coach.

Riker fired the driver's shotgun. Lane, already diving for the protection of the coach, heard the charge whistle over his head. Then he was rolling in the deep, hot dust. He was rolling toward the far side of the coach, hoping the driver could hold his teams still and that one of the ponderous, iron-tired wheels would not roll over him before he reached the other side.

There was still another charge in the shotgun, he realized. He had to get Riker before the man got him.

He reached the far side of the coach rolling, stopped and lunged to his feet. He saw Manus running toward him from the jail. He could see Riker's feet beneath the coach as the man ran toward the front of it.

He steadied himself, blinking against the dust, waiting until Riker would circle the plunging teams. He thumbed his hammer back. . . .

Riker reached the lead horses, rounded them and came plunging out into the middle of the street, shotgun held at waist level, pointed at Lane.

Down the street, Lane heard the sheriff roar, "Riker! Damn you . . . !" The sheriff fired instantly. Shot, bird shot, Lane guessed, cut through the air like a high wind. He heard it strike Riker, heard it strike the teams and, a heartbeat later, the coach itself. The teams began to plunge anew. The driver laid lack on the reins, holding their heads up by sheer brute force, giving them no choice but to rear.

Stung, Riker half-whirled. His shotgun wavered momentarily.

Lane fired instantly. He fired a second time as the impact of his first bullet made Riker trigger the gun reflexively.

The buckshot charge tore across the street diagonally, rattling on Childers' store windows. One pellet took Lane in the leg, lodging there, bringing a sudden rush of blood.

But Riker was hit. He was standing spread-legged like some gigantic tree swaying in the wind. Back and forth he swayed, the shotgun empty and pointed harmlessly at the ground. Lane watched fascinatedly, waiting for him to fall.

A red stain was spreading across the front of Riker's shirt. His throat was streaming blood. But still he stood, as though he had roots down in the dusty street.

He fell at last, ponderously, seeming almost to shake the ground.

It was over, Lane thought. Manus had stopped abruptly, the shotgun still in his hands. Suddenly, across the street, another man ran out.

It was Newkirk, inflamed by the noise and blood and violence. He had a rifle in his hands. He stood uncertainly in the middle of the street looking to right and left as though for something at which to shoot.

He spotted Childers standing in front of the furniture store. Instantly the rifle raised, and swung, and the sheriff's yell, "Newkirk!" had no noticeable effect. The rifle roared and Childers sat down suddenly as though he was very tired.

The rifle swung again and roared again, and Brooks, standing on the veranda of his hotel, was slammed back against the wall as though by the blow of a monstrous, unseen hand.

Manus, stopped in the street less than twenty feet from the man, bawled, "Drop it, Jake! Damn you, drop it or I'll shoot!"

Jake swung the gun muzzle toward Manus, his eyes completely wild. Manus fired instantly.

The charge took Newkirk squarely in the chest. It flung him back, and down into the dusty street. Up on the stagecoach seat the driver was yelling, "Stop it, goddam it! Stop that shootin'! What the hell do you think this is, the Fourth of July?"

Saralee appeared in front of the sheriff's office. White-faced, she stared toward the stagecoach, but only for an instant. Suddenly she began to run, holding up her skirts so that she wouldn't trip on them.

Her eyes were on Lane. They had been from the moment she stepped out of the jail. But she could not believe that he had come safely through all the shooting she had heard.

Ten feet away from him she stopped. She saw blood on his trouser leg and stared fearfully at his face, looking for weakness there. He managed a thin smile and said, "I'm all right, Saralee. I'm all right."

She stood there, pale and trembling. No tears came to her eyes. She said, "What now? What are you going to do?"

The smile faded. He looked around, at Riker, at Newkirk, at Brooks and Childers and Batterton.

He was thinking that the town had cleansed itself.

Enough of its citizens had taken their stand on the side of what was right to save his life. He was alive and would not have been except for conscience awakening in some of Saguaro's citizens.

His smile returned to his mouth, a gentle smile that calmed the terror in her. "Do? Nothing, I guess. I think I'll just go home."

She nodded silently, raising her eyes to look at her father on the veranda of the hotel. Lane asked, "And what will you do now?"

"I'll go to Albuquerque," she said. "I can't stay here."

A sudden awkwardness was between them, an awkwardness new to both of them. But Lane understood what it meant. He watched the color rise into her face, thinking that wherever she went, he would keep track of her. A bond was between them that nothing could ever break.

And for the first time, a smile touched Saralee's mouth. She said firmly and confidently, "Come into the hotel while I see about your leg."

Leaning on her, limping slightly, he climbed the steps to the hotel veranda and went into the lobby. He realized suddenly that the feel of menace was missing from Saguaro now. It was just another desert town drowsing in the noonday sun.